A Voodoo Shop,
A Zombie, And A Party

Deanna Oscar Paranormal Mystery, Book 4

D1713244

By CC Dragon

This book is a work of fiction. Names, characters, places, and incidents either are products of the author's imagination or are used fictitiously. Any resemblance to actual events or locales or persons, living or dead, is entirely coincidental.

A Voodoo Shop, A Zombie, And A Party (Deanna Oscar Paranormal Mystery 4)
Copyright © March 2017
By CC Dragon
Cover art by Coverkicks.com
Edited by Mary Yakovets
Proofed by: Jessica Bimberg

Dedication

For anyone who thinks they need to be strong
all the time...everyone needs help sometimes!

Table of Contents

Chapter One

You wouldn't think of the Super Bowl as a big deal at a drag club, but between the hot men in tight pants slamming into each other and the high-priced commercials on big screen TVs, The Long and Big Easy was packed. The jokes about balls and hiking the ball were getting old, but I doubted they'd slow down as people drank more.

The wait staff was dressed like cheerleaders. Most of the big TVs were on the game, but a few were switched to the Puppy Bowl or Kitten Bowl. One table actually flipped to the Harry Potter marathon. I didn't even ask. As long as they were paying customers, I didn't care, but Ivy was all out in her Super Bowl event mode.

Steve, Greg, and I were at a round booth in the back with our own personal TV. I split the screen between the human and kitten games with Tish pawing at the screen from my lap. She'd grown quickly, and I had to keep a little harness on her because she'd dart to Ivy or Greg in an instant. There were too many people to have her roaming. Ivy carried her little white dog, Pearl, like a miniature accessory, and Tish, my little black cat, could climb Ivy like a tree. She'd already shown Pearl whose claws were sharper.

I grabbed another chip from the basket of cheese-covered nachos and dodged Tish's attempt to lick it before I ate it. I did let her lick my cheesy fingers after. The truth was I'd turned out to be a cat person. Tish was smart and independent. She'd be climbing all over everyone in the room if I let her loose. Sure, she enjoyed scratches and treats, even some cuddling, but she wasn't nearly as needy as Pearl.

"That cat is going to drink your frozen margarita," Steve said with a smirk.

I moved Tish to her little bowl of water on the table then picked up my drink and sipped it. The cat wasn't buying it and pounced on my arm. Before I knew it, I had her paws on my face.

"It's the umbrella." Greg plucked it from my glass and put it in the cat's bowl. The black rescue cat jumped back to the table and was on the new toy. Tish batted at the flipping and spinning little decoration.

"Oh, halftime show!" Steve got excited.

"The halftime shows always suck. Put on the Puppy Bowl," I said.

"They replay the Puppy Bowl all night. This is live," Steve argued.

It was nice to have a guy around, sometimes. The more he was around, the more I realized the sometimes was when I was working on a case and needed an extra set of hands. Steve didn't really fit into my group naturally. Ivy didn't mind him, but he and Greg butted heads. Steve was a bit younger than me, a typical guy-next-door. Good-looking but always in jeans and a baseball hat.

"It's her bar," Greg said.

More proof Greg was smarter than Steve... Greg took my side whenever Steve wanted something else. But I couldn't be a dictator. That was a relationship. I was used to having my own way, but I didn't want to be alone forever. I'd inherited a mansion and a fortune, but I wasn't going to end up some crazy old woman in a huge house.

"Want anything from the bar?" I asked as I got up.

"What do you want? I'll get it," Steve offered.

"No, you watch the halftime show." I handed Tish to Greg. "Want anything?"

"We should probably hydrate," he said.

"Waters it is." I nodded.

I made my way to the long glass bar with shirtless men working behind it. They weren't dressed in drag but in tight jeans or leather pants. The cheerleaders were assembling on stage so they could perform as soon as the live show was over.

"Teddy. Three bottles of water and a big bowl of spicy snack mix," I said to the bartender.

"You got it. Another drink?" he asked.

"No, I'm good." I cracked open a bottle of water as soon as he set one down. Everything I'd eaten was salty, from wings to chips. "I need something sweet."

"Ivy has a cake for fourth quarter," Teddy said with a wink.

"Of course." I recapped my water and tucked the other two under my arm. I grabbed the big bowl of snack mix and turned.

Then, I froze. I sensed something before I heard it. A vision of gunfire through the massive front window filled my mind. Tires screeching could be heard from all the way out on the street.

"Get down!" I shouted. I hit the floor.

A gunshot rang out, and people gasped. Customers scrambled as glass broke. The cheerleader drag queens shrieked and dropped their trays. One wobbled on her platform heels and fell—flashing plenty of patrons. She really needed to wear Spanx!

Everyone was crawling under tables. Snack mix spilled all over. Glasses shattered when they crashed to the floor, causing more shouting that it was another shot. I braced for whatever came next. Would someone enter and demand money? What was this?

People were hugging the floor, and the chatter was gone. Muffled cries and frantic prayers could be heard, but the only loud noise was from the TVs as we waited for more shots. Nothing. We waited and stayed frozen, just in case. We all looked around at each other. No more shots rang out. Finally, the car outside sped away, and we all could take a deep breath.

"Anyone hurt?" I asked.

All the reports were negative, but a lot of people flopped into their chairs and shook their heads in shock. The few drinks still left unspilled were downed quickly. I poured myself a shot of tequila and took it, then grabbed a lime slice and sucked on it.

"Maybe it was a car backfiring?" Ivy suggested.

"Sorry, but no, boss. We got some damage." Teddy pointed to the mirror behind the bar. A bullet had cracked the glass.

"It came through the front window," Greg said.

I took the situation in slowly. The bullet would've sailed just above my head where I had been standing in front of the bar just moments ago. "I'll call Matt."

"It's probably a random thing. Misfire. Celebration." Ivy was trying so hard to sugarcoat the situation and keep on smiling in her silver and gold cheer uniform.

"The game isn't over. No one is celebrating, yet," Steve said.

"This is the French Quarter. They need to police it better if it was a random shooting," I said.

I'd been shot at before, faced snakes and murderers—but when I reached for my phone, my hand was still shaking. We needed the police one way or another. It was best I made the phone call. Matt Weathers, a bigwig detective, was working tonight. He picked up the phone for me when I dialed.

"Hey, De, what's going on?" he asked.

"Someone shot at my club," I said.

"At your place? Did you see them?" he asked.

"No, but it was pretty damn close. And it was only one shot. If they were just vandals, they'd shoot more, you'd think. I don't know. But we have a bullet, so it wasn't a car backfiring," I said.

"I'll be over with a squad. Don't touch the bullet or any evidence," he said.

Half an hour later, my patrons were annoyed about being questioned during the game. Some had left, but many weren't spooked by it. Some swore it was just a commercial and didn't want to see the bullet hole.

"Tough crowd," I said.

"New Orleans has its share of violence and gangs. We watch the French Quarter more, but there are parties all over the city. It's not quite Mardi Gras, yet. Chicago girl, your city is worse than ours," Matt said.

I smiled. "I know. But there, like New Orleans, I know where to go and where not to. This is supposed to be a safe area. Touristy. The biggest thing I should worry about is pickpockets. One bullet isn't gangs. They'd shoot the place to hell and back. Someone is sending a message."

"One bullet. Is that random or well-placed?" Greg frowned at the broken mirror.

"Probably a kid got his dad's gun and was showing off to friends. Getting drunk in the French Quarter. This is the night everyone is in somewhere watching the game. Eyes are glued to the big screens. Teens sometimes run a bit wild and do stupid stuff because the adults are all distracted. The kids have already watched all the commercials on the Internet. and they watch the games on their phone or tablet. They don't care about a big screen." Matt sighed. His family owned the mansion across the street from mine. His brother was a judge, and another brother was a lawyer. He knew this city deep down, from gangs and kids to the rich and powerful.

"You're probably right. If someone wanted to shoot me, they'd have hit me. None of us saw it coming. We hit the ground when we heard tires. Then it was the shot and glass breaking. It just felt too close." I rubbed my forehead.

"You need another drink." Ivy poured me a shot. "Drink."

"No, I'm fine." I looked down at the scattered snack mix. The bottles of water had skidded who knows where. The staff was cleaning up spills all over.

"We'll document everything, I've got squads circling the block and moving out farther to see. Odds are the kids scared themselves and ran off. I'll write up a report for your insurance. I'd duct tape the glass and buy a new mirror." Matt shrugged.

I nodded and downed the shot. "I hope that's all it is." I knew it wasn't. Being psychic had disadvantages. I couldn't explain my instincts or feelings. There was no proof. But someone meant to shoot into my club. Did they want to kill me or someone else? Was it some other warning? I wasn't sure, yet, but I had to take the message seriously.

Greg put Tish on my shoulder. The purring cat helped me relax a bit.

"It's nothing," Steve said.

Greg was an ex-priest who'd worked with my grandmother. He looked the part in dress slacks and a dress shirt now with rolled up sleeves. He was older than me and had that distinguished something about him you couldn't pin down.

The best thing about him was that he didn't make assumptions. He looked at me. "Was it?"

I shook my head. Like it or not, I had to trust my annoying but accurate psychic powers. "It was intentional."

I had plans for investigation the next day, but sometimes, even I couldn't predict what would happen. I woke to Mary Lou Weathers, my friend from across the street who happened to be Matt's sister-in-law, dragging me out of bed with Ivy at her side.

Ivy lived with me. She and Greg, her cousin, had moved in when I moved up to Chicago to look after my brother. What I had hoped was a short visit had ended up being years, and at least my house was occupied. When you have house ghosts roaming, bad ghosts locked up in the attic, and a possessed object under the stairs— you couldn't just leave a house standing empty.

The big mansion felt better with Ivy and Greg in it so I'd asked them to stay. I wasn't born into rich high society so all that space to myself was eerie. Mary Lou, however, loved the riches, and if I ever needed a lesson in how to spend my money, she'd happily volunteer.

"Spa day," Mary Lou insisted.

"No, I have to find out about the shooting. I'm not feeling great either," I said.

"More reason to pamper yourself. You need a fresh set of nails, and your eyebrows need a little wax," Ivy said.

"And a hair trim. I see split ends," Mary Lou sighed. "You get too wrapped up in work, and you don't take care of yourself."

"Not everyone is a beauty pageant queen," I said.

Mary Lou had been Miss Louisiana back in her day. I could pull myself together for a wedding or other formal event, but my job was not about looks.

"When you look better, you feel better," Ivy said.

"Even if you have a boyfriend, you have to keep him interested," Mary Lou added.

I rolled my eyes. If Steve didn't like the way I looked, he could get lost. I kept myself up well, but I didn't have three hours a day to primp and pluck.

"Come on. Mani/pedis and a little trim." Ivy nodded.

"Fine. I could use a day off, I guess," I said.

I hadn't been working all that much, but with the shooting, I'd be breathing down Matt's neck. He probably sent Mary Lou over to distract me so he had a day to find out who did it.

Still, an hour later I was at a spa. The day started with pedicures.

"So, do you think Steve is the one?" Mary Lou asked.

"I don't know. It's not that serious," I said.

"You're never serious about guys," Ivy said.

"The Ghost Tamer thing was all your fault, Ivy. I never wanted to be on a TV show or work with another team. So, it's all on you. He's not a bad guy. I really needed a date for the wedding, and he was there. But we're both busy, and I'm not working with that group, again. I don't want my stuff all over TV," I said.

"Nothing wrong with privacy. You're the real deal. Their show is a bit cheesy," Mary Lou admitted.

"It's very popular. I'm trying to make you as popular as you deserve, De. People need to hear your message. See what you can do," Ivy said.

"Message? What message? I'm not broadcasting advice, Ivy. I just want to help people who need it. Everyone in America doesn't need to see what I do or how. I don't need the money. Gran left me well off, and I've been watching the investments. I made some good moves with Eddie's advice while I was in Chicago. Grew the money. We don't need to worry. And you've got the club making a nice profit, too," I said.

"True. I just always feel like we should be doing more. Helping more people or letting them know we're here to help. I know you don't like being a minor New Orleans celebrity, but that's how people find out about you."

"She does have a point there," Mary Lou said.

"Matt brings me to the attention of people who need me. Weird cases I'm good with. Greg can bring me cases from different angles. He's working more with the demonologists and stuff. It's good for him," I said.

"It is. But now, you're sort of flying solo, and you need work," Ivy said.

"I don't need work. Work finds me. Plus, I have to figure out who shot at the club," I said.

"So awful. Stressful and senseless. Ruining people's evenings with one bullet." Mary Lou shook her head.

The conversation broke slightly while we switched to manicures.

"Any guys around for you, Ivy?" I asked.

"I thought you were dating someone," Mary Lou said.

"No, I gave up on him. Some men can't handle a woman with a demanding job. He wanted me there all the time on his arm. I've got my own big career. That club doesn't run itself.

So, he got sick of me not putting him first all the time. Done."

"You made the right choice. You can put a guy first, and he loves it. But if you have to come first for any amount of time, it's like you attacked them. In the end, most of them just leave, anyway. I saw it so many times in grad school," I said.

"Even if he is rich enough to spoil you, you need to find your own things. Have your own life. Men." Mary Lou sipped her fancy coffee drink.

Mary Lou married Luke Weathers, a rich lawyer. Their marriage was less than ideal, but she was a trophy wife, and he was a rich guy. Somehow, they made it work. I did my best not to judge. Rumors of infidelity on both sides made me stay off that topic unless she brought it up. But it did remind me that there were worse things than being single, even at my age.

Once our nails were done, mine a classic French tip on gel nails, I was pushed into the shampoo chair. First, the girl did my eyebrows, then washed my long black hair. I couldn't remember exactly when my last haircut was... Chicago, definitely. But my hair was long, and it didn't look shabby. I wasn't one for a ton of makeup, just the basics. As I'd aged, there were more and more basics, but I maintained a size twelve, and other than a few more crow's feet, I was holding up okay.

The stylist took off an inch and angled things here and there, but it wasn't much. I could barely tell the difference. Before I even stood, the hair had been swept away. It was the cleanest spa I'd ever been to. The priciest, as well.

"Don't you feel better?" Mary Lou asked.

"I do. Now, let me treat you guys to lunch since you dragged me out," I said.

"Somewhere with salads, please," Mary Lou said.

"One day, you're going to turn into a salad," I teased.

"We all don't get our cardio chasing ghosts," Mary Lou shot back.

"Come dancing at the club. It's great, and the men are gay so your hubby can't get mad," Ivy advised.

"I'll be there for the Mardi Gras party. If I go out too much, I hear it from my mother-in-law. High society and all that crap. I have charity events to attend. Boards to sit on. It's so boring," Mary Lou said.

"See, you're stuck working...rich hubby or not," I said.

"I'm holding out for Mr. Perfect, not just Mr. Right," Ivy said.

"How do you know the good from the bad without wasting a lot of time on them?" I asked.

"If you feel like you're wasting any time, he's the wrong one," Ivy said.

I nodded and decided to head to my favorite seafood place. They had salad, and their fried shrimp was to die for. Those two could eat healthy if they wanted, but I needed some comfort food, especially if we were going to be discussing my joke of a love life.

Chapter Two

There hadn't been any more gunfire since the big game. But a storm rolled through New Orleans overnight, and I woke with a pressure headache and tension in my shoulders.

Was it just the weather or part of the dark cloud that felt like was following me?

"Maybe Mercury is retrograde?" Ivy asked as she fussed.

The cucumbers on my eyes weren't helping. The eggs that Missy, my house ghost, was cooking turned my stomach.

"She's pregnant," Greg said with a chuckle.

"Don't even. Shut up." Ivy hugged me.

"No, no. Not possible. This is like migraine nausea." I grabbed a piece of toast. "Do we have any sea sickness pills?"

"No. Just headache stuff." Ivy sorted through the pill cabinet.

"I'll get you some. I have a house out in the boonies that needs cleaning today," Greg said.

Ivy propped her hand on her hip. "Wait. You and Steve haven't...?"

"No. What do you think I am?" I grabbed the aspirin bottle from her.

"More fun than that." Ivy rolled her eyes.

"No, I'm not fun. I'm not that easy either. I'll go with you, Greg. We can stop for pills and a big water on the way." I finished the toast and some coffee, but the dark cloud and pain were still there.

"Okay. Sure you're up for it?" he asked.

"I can help or sit in the car. Ivy has to get to the club and I need the pills or vertigo will get me. I'm not going up the stairs like this."

"Maybe you need to see a doctor." Ivy felt my forehead.

"No, it's just a headache trying to be a migraine. No other symptoms. It happens." I rubbed my neck.

"Luckily, this house I'm going to cleanse isn't full-on demon possessed, but there is a lot of dead attracted to the it. I think the teenage boy that lives there is creating a poltergeist. Puberty and energy. Plus, he has this thing for bugs." Greg shook his head.

"Bugs?" I asked.

"He collects and analyzes them. Maybe he'll be a scientist," Greg said.

"Or an exterminator," Ivy added.

"So, you're blessing the house and trying to remove the growing poltergeist?" I asked.

"More or less, but the kid needs to stop feeding it. He bottles his emotions and that strengthens it." Greg checked his phone.

"What's the plan? You cleanse the house; I talk to the kid?" I asked.

"I'll talk to him. You find where it's hiding."

"Sounds like a demon if it's hiding." Ivy dug into her eggs.

"It's at an early stage where it's just acting on survival. And the kid made it, so no, not a demon. But if it grows and gains too much energy, it could act on what the kid wants without the kid's intention."

"In other words, it's big trouble," I said.

"Have fun with that." Ivy toasted us with a glass of orange juice.

We were outside of the city limits, that was for sure. The homes were far apart and very old with siding fall off. I was glad that Greg was keeping busy. As a former priest he had done exorcisms officially and had been trained but left his vows. Being raised Catholic, I knew the church wasn't perfect but this new pope made me have more hope. However, when it came to casting gout demons Catholics had the training, the tools, and the discretion.

Greg knocked on the door and I stood behind him. The vertigo pills were working, but I still felt like it was a gloomy overcast day. The reality was a blue sky and sun so bright I was lucky I'd found my sunglasses in my purse.

A woman opened the door and eyed me uneasily. "Needed more help?" she asked.

"Deanna will make it much easier to track the anomaly," Greg said. "Deanna Oscar, Mrs. Rhendi. Her son is Pierce."

I smiled at the African American woman in a house dress and flats. She didn't look old enough to have a son that tall.

"She needs to see the house?" Mrs. Rhendi asked.

"You can give her the tour, but she'll find the problem on her own, if you'd rather step outside." Greg set up in the kitchen.

The house wasn't large. The living room and kitchen were clear. I followed Mrs. Rhendi back to the bedrooms. Hers was calm, and she had enough crosses in there that I flashed on that creepy episode of Game of Thrones where a ridiculously long row of people were crucified. Thanks, Mr. Martin, for reminding us that the cross wasn't just for Jesus.

"My son's room is back there. I hope you don't mind bugs," she said.

I smiled. "Greg mentioned he was a collector and studied them. Are they contained?" I asked.

"Mostly in jars, but he has an ant farm or two." She nodded.

"I won't touch anything." I waited for her to go in first, like she had with the rest of the rooms.

"You can go on in. It's a small room. Not much free space," she said.

"Okay." I turned the knob and entered.

There was a weird noise only bugs make. Not quite a scuttling, but it made me shudder. The wiggling was hard to ignore. Everywhere I looked, there were jars full of squirming bugs. Roaches, ants, centipedes, weird bugs in water, and more were bad enough. When I saw the spider shelf, I caught my foot on the bed. "Damn."

"You okay in there?" Mrs. Rhendi called.

"Yeah. But you're right about the tight space. I didn't expect the spiders." I took in the variety. Tiny and sleek to huge and furry.

"He loves those things. His specialty," she said.

"They aren't technically bugs, but not the point." I tried to shake off the gloom and the creepy crawly feel. The focus of Pierce's anxiety and frustration was in the closet.

I slid the door open and found the light, concerned about the bugs that might be in there. Then, my eye caught the swirling entity in the corner.

"Find it?" Greg asked from the doorway.

"Closet. Want to trade places?" I asked.

"That's the plan," he said.

I slid back toward the door as he walked in. I leaned back to give him room and, to my horror, bumped the spider shelf.

Greg grabbed something behind me, and I ducked out of the room fast. "Sorry."

"You're good. Nothing broke." Greg went to work like it was all normal.

He was a native and used to the weird bugs, snakes, and alligators that Louisiana boasted. Chicago had snakes and bugs, but nothing that could kill you.

I scratched my neck and shoulders. It was psychosomatic, of course. All the wiggly bugs.

"I don't know how he sleeps in that room." Mrs. Rhendi shook her head.

"I like them. They make sense," Pierce said. He had appeared out of nowhere, adding to the creepy factor of the whole situation. The boy standing just behind her was a bean pole with a serious expression.

"But there are so many. They never escape?" I asked.

He shrugged. "Sometimes, but all of them are native. Maybe they escaped. Maybe it's a new bug who made its way into the house."

I couldn't think about that. I ran my fingers through my hair again to be sure. But, really, I needed to help Pierce refocus some of his energy to balance things out and diminish the entity in his closet.

"Do you do any sports or dance?" I asked.

He laughed. "I'm going to college so I can buy my mom a fancy house."

Mrs. Rhendi beamed with pride.

"That's great, and I hear your grades are amazing. But you might want to balance it out a bit. The emotions and frustrations that build up, you need to let them out in a physical way. Even if it's just turning up the music and dancing with your mom." I walked out into the living room and felt instantly better, except for my neck.

The wiggly sensation wouldn't stop. Even though it was all in my mind, I scratched and smacked at my neck.

"I feel that way every time I go in there to clean." Mrs. Rhendi patted my shoulder.

I tugged the sweater away from my skin to let the cool air calm it. But something fell from the fabric.

I stomped on the whatever it was out of instinct. When I picked up my foot, there was a brown spider squished on the floor.

"Oh, crap," Pierce said.

"Why 'oh, crap'?" I asked.

"It must've fallen in your hair or down your collar. How did it get out?" Pierce asked.

"What is it? Is it bad?" I didn't know what I was looking at.

"They don't normally bite," Pierce said.

I pulled the neck of my shirt down and touched my skin.

"You won't feel the pain right away. But you should get to the hospital," Pierce continued.

"Greg!" I shrieked.

"In a minute," he called back.

"Why the hospital?" I asked Pierce.

Mrs. Rhendi bent down and looked at the spider. "That's a brown recluse. And you've got a little red spot on your neck like it did get you."

"It's probably just me scratching." I prodded the area with my nails and it was tender.

Greg walked out. "What's the emergency?" he asked.

"Spider bite. Chicago spiders don't send you to the hospital." I frowned.

He looked down. "A recluse? Hell," he said.

"You better take her in to be sure," Mrs. Rhendi said.

"You're right. We'll go to the ER," he said.

"No, not the ER. Just make a doctor's appointment," I said.

"I don't think too long of a wait is a good idea. Let's go." Greg nudged me out toward the front door.

"Better take the specimen." Pierce used tweezers to put the dead arachnid into a small jar. Greg put the lid on tight and handed it to me.

I got in the car, and the rush of warmth on my neck irritated the slightly swollen bite mark. Holding up the jar, I stared at my tiny attacker.

The cloud over my life was getting darker and larger.

I sat in the ER waiting room as Ivy tried to find a clinic that could squeeze me in rather than sit at the hospital all day.

"Damn!" Ivy tossed her phone at her purse.

"I'll be fine." I scratched my neck.

"Stop scratching. You'll get it infected." Ivy smacked my hand away.

"It itches. I need water." I stood and went in search of a vending machine or drinking fountain.

A man in a white coat carrying a sports drink crossed my path. I knew him. He was wearing the wrong coat, but it was him. I turned.

"Death?" I asked.

He turned. "Are you okay, miss?"

"Doctor," I said.

"Yes, I'm a doctor. I thought you said death," he replied.

It was him. "Yes, you're Death. I'm a doctor. I'm thirsty. And itchy."

"Miss, why are you here?" he asked.

"Doctor," I insisted as my mind grew a bit foggier.

"Yes, I'm a doctor."

"No, you're Death. I'm a doctor. Don't you recognize me? You were stalking me and my brother not that long ago." I touched my neck. "I hate spiders. Why couldn't it be snakes? I can handle snakes from a distance."

"Okay, Doctor. Are you waiting to see a doctor?" he asked.

"Yes, a medical one. Why else would I be here? I got bite by some brown thingy. I don't like it." I put dollars into the machine and pushed buttons until it gave me water.

"You were bitten by a brown recluse?" He looked at my neck. "That's a slow-acting but nasty venom."

"Tell me to go home," I said.

"Not quite. Let's get you back in a room to be sure you're not having an allergic reaction. I see some blotching developing, now. When were you bitten?" he asked.

He led me back to the waiting area. "What time is it now?" I asked

"Who is with Miss..." he prompted me.

"Doctor! Dr. Deanna Oscar, PhD," I said too loud.

The concerned looks on Ivy and Greg's faces told me I wasn't as together as I thought I was.

"Is it bad?" Ivy asked.

"She's definitely not herself," Greg said. "I was with her."

"We just want to get her on a monitor and be sure she's not going into anaphylactic shock. I'm Dr. Brimlow."

A nurse came over with a wheelchair, and I didn't argue about getting into it. They wheeled me back, but all the rooms were taken. I was put on a bed in the packed hallway.

"She has good insurance," Ivy huffed.

Suddenly, I had patches on my chest and a clip on my finger. Someone was taking my blood pressure while someone else stuck a thermometer in my mouth.

The doctor returned as the nurses walked away. "I looked at the spider your friend had. It's a brown recluse. It'll hurt and blister. It'll eat away at the skin, so you'll want to see your doctor every day for the next five days to be safe.

Tylenol for the pain and ice for the swelling. Benadryl for itching. I'll give you antibiotics to prevent the open wound from getting infected. But I want to make sure you don't have a systemic reaction. Some people are allergic."

"How will you know?" I asked.

He took out a Sharpie and drew on my neck.

"What the hell?" I asked.

"Marking the swelling and blotching. We'll see how fast it spreads, but it's already spread far faster than the average bite. We'll get you some Benadryl and an epi pen. Just sit still," he said.

"You don't remember me?" I asked.

He smiled. "Sorry. I'm just a doctor. Not the Angel of Death."

"Damn." I sat back.

The place was so packed that you had to be having a heart attack to get a room. A new patient was wheeled into the hall space next to me. She wore a tiara that said "Bride" and a sash that announced it as well. She and the friends who had tagged along were drunk and giggling, despite the Bachelorette Beauty Queen sporting a bloody foot.

"That looks bad," I said.

"We have one doc who just does stitches. But she does need a lot. Are you okay?" Dr. Brimlow asked me.

I nodded. Then, a man wearing nothing but skintight blue pants and a policeman's gun belt and hat came in with cheesy stripper music coming from his phone. He shimmied up to the ladies, and they shrieked as only the thoroughly inebriated could.

"Bachelorette party this early?" I asked.

"Honey, we're still going from last night. Wedding isn't until tomorrow!" shouted one of the bridesmaids.

A nurse asked them to turn down the music as she approached my bedside, and they did a bit, but it was bringing back my headache.

"That man can move," Ivy observed.

I drank some more water as the nurse gave me a shot and some pills.

He was hot, but I wasn't in the mood for anything but sleep until I felt normal again.

The stripper was bumping, grinding, and annoying most of the people in the crowded hallway. He held his phone up in the air like he did exotic dancing in hospitals every day.

I closed my eyes, leaned back on the bed and imagined my finger deleting the music app on his phone.

The music suddenly stopped.

I sat up. "Are my ears ringing?"

"What happened?" The stripper hit his phone over and over. "The app won't work."

The bridesmaids were puzzled and pouting.

The bride waved him over. "Come hold me while they stitch up my foot."

The stripper sat next to her.

Ivy looked at me.

I shrugged. Then, I saw that my guardian angel had shown up.

"Was that you?" I asked Amy the Angel. Technically, Amy wasn't her real name but she didn't want to share. Angels were hard to talk to.

She shook her head.

"Who?" I asked.

"You okay, De?" Ivy asked.

"Shh, I'm talking to my angel." I patted Ivy's hand.

"You turned off the music. Your powers are expanding," replied the angel.

"Don't tell me the spider gave me weird powers. I'm not going to turn into a spiderwoman, am I?" I rubbed my forehead.

Greg left quickly and came back with the doctor.

"Dr. Oscar, are you with us?" Dr. Brimlow asked.

"Sure. I'm fine." I shrugged.

"You asked if you were going to be Spiderwoman?" he asked.

"Not to you. This isn't about you." I waved him away.

"I think we should keep you overnight for observation," the doc said.

"No, no. I'm feeling better. The Benadryl kicked in." I rubbed my neck. "I was just talking to my angel."

"She's a psychic medium. Not crazy," Ivy said.

"Angels? Psychics? This is normal?" the doc asked Greg.

"Very normal for her. The drugs and spider venom are confusing her. Normally, she juggles this stuff like it's nothing. We'll make sure she rests and sees a doctor for the next few days." Greg nodded.

The doc pulled out his prescription pad. "Benadryl, Tylenol, and this antibiotic. Gently wash the wound and cover until the doc sees her tomorrow. Don't try to pop the blister."

"Do you have a card?" I asked.

He fished one out of his pocket. "You should have a GP."

"I don't. I want you." I handed him my card.

"I'll call you later and sort out your aftercare. Give you a referral." He pocketed my card.

"I want house calls," I said.

"De, stop sounding crazy," Ivy hissed.

"I'm serious. I can pay." I stood to leave.

"You have to leave in a wheelchair. Hospital rules," the doc said.

I sighed and waited for the chair. When I finally got a ride, I turned and found Ivy flirting with the stripper. She was always Ivy. I smiled at Greg.

"Come on, Ivy. You have to play nurse with me. Not a stripper nurse, a real nurse," I said.

Ivy laughed. "That's Greg and Steve's job."

"Not Steve, I don't want him to see me like this. I feel funky. I need more water." I smacked my tongue like I had been without water for hours.

Greg handed me a bottle of water. "Make it last until we get home."

I nodded as I opened the bottle. I kept it to sips as they wheeled me out the door. I looked back at the doc again. He looked just like Death had. It had to be the drugs and spider bite.

I closed my eyes. I'd sort it out later.

Chapter Three

My morning headache was a vacation compared to the throbbing in my head and the pain in my neck and shoulder area. Ivy changed the ice pack, and I was grateful for my friends who'd kept me safe and sane.

"Thanks." I was sleepy from the meds.

"Greg is getting your antibiotic from the pharmacy. I'm going to call that doc and have him make a house call tomorrow. Give me the card," Ivy said.

I reached for my pocket and winced. Why did I put it on the same side as the bite?

"I'll get it." She dug her hand in my pocket and pulled it out. "You should get into a nightgown, anyway. You need to sleep this off."

"Why me? I swear, something is off," I said.

"Hon, you got bit by a spider in a house full of creepy crawly things. It's not exactly the ten plagues of Egypt. I mean, it's serious. We're going to watch you and get that doc out here daily, but don't get paranoid. The blotching stopped, and the swelling is going down. Just keep up the dosing of meds on time and lots of water." Ivy took a picture of the business card with her phone.

She took a pic of another card, as well. I was pretty sure it was the stripper's card. Ivy lived on her phone, and she'd lose the cards eventually, so it was safer. I almost asked what she wanted with the stripper, but she might tell me more than I wanted to know, right now.

"When do I get paranoid?" I shot back at her.

Ivy had changed from her drag attire for the club to jeans and a t-shirt. She still wanted to be female despite not being trans, in or out of drag. I just went with it. Clothes were just clothes. Right now, she was dressed like I usually did. I just couldn't imagine dressing up like she did daily.

"Not often, but I've rarely seen you sick or hurt. You had a headache, and now, you have a medical situation. Don't blow it out of proportion. You're not immortal." She looked at her phone. "Do you think that stripper was cute?"

"Your nursing skills are lacking. Did you actually take care of my grandmother as a medical aide?" I teased.

"I was very good when that was my job. Now, I run your club. Now, I'm just acting as your friend. You don't need a full-time nurse. Your grandmother insisted on doing everything she could on her own. She never thought anyone had put a whammy on her to make her weak or block her gifts." Ivy chuckled.

"Why are you talking about the stripper, anyway?" I jumped back to her question. My brain was still too foggy to be linear, at the moment.

"He's hot. I lost a bartender. Guess the bullet got too close for him." She shrugged.

"But I was overreacting about the shooting?" I folded my arms and regretted it immediately as pain shot through my arm.

"Another dose of Tylenol is due. You need to keep taking it on schedule, because that is going to get worse before it's better." Ivy shook out the pills

I swallowed them without complaint. "Do we want a stripper working the bar?"

"He's hot, and maybe he could use some regular work. He can still strip on the side." She smiled at her phone.

"You're texting with him, now?" I concluded.

"Yep. He's gay and likes our club. I'll interview him tomorrow." She put her phone in her pocket. "Now, about the doc. You called him Death. Are you okay with that doctor? I can get you another one."

"He looks like Death. Remember that guy?" I asked.

Ivy frowned. "I remember a guy who was hanging around, and you said he was Death. But I don't remember him looking like that. The doc is cute but...not familiar to me."

"Okay. Maybe I'm losing it." I rubbed my eyes.

"No, you had venom running through your veins that you're allergic to. He might look familiar, so I'm going to get you some lunch. No arguing. Greasy cheeseburgers and curly fries." Ivy winked.

"Strawberry milkshake?" I asked.

"You got it. But stay in bed and nap," she said.

I nodded. "Okay."

Ivy left and closed the door behind her. I couldn't sleep. I wasn't crazy. I waited until I was sure she'd left and I was alone in the house before I gave in to my curiosity.

"Death!" I said firmly. "I need the Angel of Death to show up, now, or I'm coming to find you."

Gran showed up. "How would you do that?"

"I'd project to Heaven and track Death from there. Not sure how I'd get to him, but I need to know I'm not crazy." I took a drink of water.

"Fine. You need to rest. You're not crazy about any of it." My dead grandmother turned as if to leave.

"How's Eddie?" I asked quickly.

"Recovering. Don't worry about him. You've got real problems." Gran vanished.

"Is it me or is she getting less helpful?" I asked no one in particular.

The room was empty, but I knew now it never really was.

"Amy, Angel Amy...don't ignore me. I don't like that," I said. She and I had formed a tense peace ever since I'd met her. She'd never shown up during my entire confusing childhood, so I had a chip on my shoulder a bit. But I was willing to take her help.

She grudgingly appeared. "Your grandmother can't give you any and all information you'd like.

She is busy with your brother, as well. You don't need to worry about him."

"I didn't call for her. I was looking for Death. Where is Death? Death!" I called.

"We don't do your bidding," the angel said.

"No, you work for the big guy, I know. But you have no free will, and I can be extremely annoying if I have to be to get the results I want. Death, you let a spider bite me. Am I on the list? I'll interrupt you day and night. I know you can hear me." I must've pushed the right combination of buttons.

But it wasn't the cute doc from today in that sharp suit I remembered him wearing from before.

It was a black lady with dreadlocks in a brightly colored house dress.

"Who is this?" I asked Amy.

"Who is dis?" Death said with a heavy Jamaican accent. "I'm Death. Who do ya think you've been callin' for? Shoutin' your head off annoys more den me."

"But Death was that guy before. Something is wrong." I pressed my temples.

"Death is an angel who wears a body. It's a borrowed body. I know I explained it to ya before. I'm still me, just borrowin' a different body." Death shrugged.

"But the guy. That was him, the doctor. So, he doesn't remember his body being used by Death?" I asked.

"Mos' bodies we borrow are from people who are decidin'. Dere in a coma or otherwise in limbo if dey'll return to life or die. Dey might remember some things, but most don't. Some remember a near death experience, but dos tend to be quick. He was in a coma. But dis doctor had to be a good person if an angel used his body. If dat makes ya feel good," she said.

"I'm just glad I'm not crazy. I saw him today. What are the odds?" I asked.

"Extraordinary. This woman is currently in a hospital in Kingston, Jamaica," my angel said.

I slid from the bed and walked over. "But I can touch her. She's real. People see her." I tapped Death on the shoulder.

"Yes," my angel said.

"And her body's not missing from the hospital?" I asked.

"No," Death answered.

"That makes no sense," I said.

"Don't question the man upstairs. Maybe I'm tryin' out the afterlife. Maybe Death needs a way to talk to people." Death smiled. "Ya aren't crazy, woman. And no, yer not on my list. A little spider bite won't kill ya as long as ya get dose medical checks. But dat's not the only issue."

The doorbell rang.

"What's the other issue?" I asked.

The doorbell rang, again, more insistently this time.

Damn! "I have to go. Greg and Ivy are both out. We'll pick this up later."

"Ya don' dictate to me, Missy," Death said.

I pointed to myself. "Free will." I pointed to them. "No free will. I'm just a puny human with a spider bite, but I'll use what I've got to get answers and some help when I need it."

On adrenaline or annoyance, I walked down the stairs. Halfway down, I got a little tired and leaned on the ornately carved handrail. I had a lovely mansion in the Garden District, but sometimes, the house was just too freaking big!

The doorbell rang, again. I knew it was Matt, and whatever it was, it was important.

"I'm coming!" I shouted.

I made it to the bottom of the stairs and suddenly felt weak. Taking a deep breath, I waved my hand, and the door unlocked.

New powers. New problems. But I waved my hand, again, and the door opened.

Matt looked in. "Ghosts answering the door?"

"No, me. I need to sit down." I stumbled into the kitchen and eased into a chair.

"You look like hell. I got a text about a spider bite." Matt leaned over my neck. "Looks small so far."

"I guess I'm a little allergic to that spider. I'll be fine. What's up?" I asked.

Matt pointed to the fridge. "Mind if I?"

"Help yourself." I shrugged.

He pulled out a pitcher of lemonade and poured two glasses. After he put the pitcher away, he grabbed an apple from the fruit bowl and washed it, then chopped it into slices.

"Snack." He set a glass and the apple in front of me.

"Ivy is getting us cheeseburgers," I said.

"Your body is fighting off poison. Eat. Then, I'll explain why I'm here." He sat and sipped from his own glass.

After a couple of apple slices, I felt a bit more normal. I frowned when I sipped the lemonade. "Weird combo."

"I'm not a chef. Now, have you heard about the Trailer Park Three?" Matt asked.

"No. Is that some band? I really don't like country music." I grabbed a piece of cornbread from the plate in the middle of the table, Missy always had some bread or pastry on hand, and I needed some to balance my taste buds.

He laughed. "You are out of it. You think I'd come over here and bug you while you're looking like hell if it was about some honkytonk band and I've got an extra ticket to their concert?"

"Fine. Enlighten me. I don't watch the news. It's too depressing," I said.

"Three girls, all freshmen in high school. All live in the Rivette trailer park. They went to the same Super Bowl party together and a friend saw them all leave together. The three reportedly got into an Uber to go home." Matt sighed.

"They didn't make it home," I said.

"No, they didn't. But the parents didn't panic, right away. The girls were close friends and stayed at each other's homes all the time. They assumed they spent the night at one of the other girl's homes. The parents were at parties of their own, so take that for what it's worth. If they were hungover or tired, they might have been less apt to notice. Either way, it wasn't until noon the next day that one of the mothers started calling around for her daughter. The girls' cell phones are all dead. We've been searching for two days." He glanced at me to gauge my reaction.

Normally, I'd have a sense or feeling immediately. I had answers or at least a direction to move in.

I had nothing.

"Uber records?" I asked.

"It wasn't an Uber, apparently. We've got a vague description of the car they got into but no plate info. They were drunk kids not paying attention. But the girls got in the car willingly, no struggle. We know that much," Matt added.

"I thought kids didn't care about football. Isn't that your theory of who shot at my club?" I asked.

"Some kids look for any excuse to party. Some kids are loners. These girls have families who are worried to death. The moms are good. They didn't let their girls go alone, gave them money for an Uber, and they all had cell phones to call for help or a ride. These were good girls. No trouble at school. No history of running away. They aren't rich. No one in the Garden District is putting up reward money, but these girls didn't put themselves in a bad situation. Are they dead?" he asked.

"I need pictures or something. More than a sad news tagline." I finished off my lemonade and tapped the glass on the table.

"You are annoying when you're not well." Matt flipped through the papers in his folder then slapped a picture of the girls on the table and grabbed my glass.

"I'm just acting like my brothers and dad did anytime they were sick. Spider bite is at least equal to man flu." I focused on the picture.

Matt refilled my lemonade.

"Thanks." I sipped the cool liquid. "Checked with other friends to be sure?"

"I know how to do my job. I wouldn't be here if I had another lead." Matt helped himself to cornbread. "Want their names?"

I shook my head. I closed my eyes and put my hand on the picture. The room flipped on me. I was even more tired and weak. Something smelled awful. The room went up and down like it was on the water. Maybe they were on a boat? I couldn't focus in on them.

I tried to get into one of the girls' heads and make her open her eyes for an accurate picture. She tried, but then, someone pushed a needle in her arm.

"They're alive. They're drugged and being held somewhere. Near the water." I pushed the picture away.

"That narrows it down."

"Sorry, I'm not at full steam, and there is a ton of water around here. Put me in a car, and I can start to get a direction. Right now, all I've got is head toward the bayou." I rubbed my shoulders.

The door opened, and Ivy walked in.

"Oh, hell no. She is supposed to be in bed and resting. Matt, out." Ivy put the promised bag of food on the table.

Chapter Four

"Where's my shake?" I asked.

Ivy set down a drink carrier, and I grabbed the cup like an eager kid. I was sick—I had to admit it, and it made me feel like a kid.

"Hey, I fed her and got her lemonade. You shouldn't have left her alone," Matt said.

"I'm fine. You can all leave," I said.

"You're making her work. Dragging her down the stairs. Matt, she gets a sick day or three once in a while. Leave her alone. Out," Ivy said.

I dug through the bag and found my cheeseburger.

"She's fighting off the venom. She needs good food. Lots of healthy snacks and water to keep her strength up." Matt eyed my lunch. "Not junk."

"You know about spider bites?" Ivy rolled her eyes and pulled a big bag of fries out of the greasy bag.

I grabbed some fries. "Thank you."

Matt huffed. "I do. We had a cousin who got bit five times at once. Old shack on her daddy's property was overrun by the recluses. They don't go after people, but she was trying to get something off a shelf in a closet, and they fell down her dress. Poor thing still has the scars."

"Fine. Regular snacks. Lots of water. Pills on time. I'll handle it. Greg needs to get back with the antibiotics." Ivy looked at her watch.

"It takes time to fill them. He had the script with him." I appreciated the attention, but they were fussing too much.

"I know. But you're not going off on any case without those antibiotics and a babysitter. I was going to leave you here with Missy. At home, a ghost can make sure you have snacks, water, and that you take your pills. But not if you're working," Ivy said.

"I can take care of myself." I felt better because I was eating, again.

"No. Greg has a job later. I have to get to the club," Ivy said.

The doorbell rang. "Damn," she grumbled.

Matt glanced at me as if I knew who it was. I shrugged.

Ivy returned from answering the door with a small bag in one hand and that stripper guy from the emergency room following her.

"Hi," I said.

"Ma'am. Glad to see you're feeling better." He tipped an imaginary hat.

"Greg dropped these off. He had to go. Now, you eat. I'm going to talk to Gunnar in the living room," Ivy said.

"Gunnar?" I asked. "I thought you were meeting tomorrow."

"I was free, now, and Miss Ivy said the sooner the better," Gunnar said.

"I thought I recognized you," Matt said.

"Hi." Gunnar blushed.

"Gay strippers?" I looked at Matt.

"No, he was a beat cop for a couple years. Stripping?" Matt asked.

Gunner lifted a shoulder. "The pay is better. The uniform gave me an idea, and it was crazy popular."

"Sex and drugs sell." Matt sighed.

"I don't do either of those. Just legal stuff," Gunnar said.

"Why did you leave the force?" I asked.

"The other cops made fun of me when they learned what I was doing on the side. Then, they found out how much I charged. Eventually, I realized someone else needed that cop job. And some of the parties get a little wild. Other people bring drugs, and I didn't want to be picked up while I was on the force," Gunnar said.

"Bartending work is legit. Not that stripping isn't, but it involves less pelvic thrusting. Let's chat." Ivy crooked a finger at Gunnar.

They left the room, and I munched on my fries. "Small world."

Matt shook his head. "Good cops are hard to find and keep."

"Hazard pay?" I slurped on my shake.

He glared at me.

"Most cops don't look like him," I teased and scratched my neck.

"Don't touch." He batted my hand away. "You don't want to mess with that."

"I hate your critters down here," I said.

"You like snow and ice better?" he asked.

I nodded. "Snow and ice kill these things. Bug-free winter."

"You're moving back?" he challenged.

I frowned. "That's not my call. I have to stay where I'm supposed to be."

"Your choice." He grabbed a fry.

I nodded. It was my choice. I had the choice, but I knew I couldn't do what I needed to do with my parents in the same city. I wouldn't feel free enough to use my skills. I had to have the breathing space.

"Do you think you can find those girls?" he asked.

"I want to try. They can't get loose. They're tied up and being drugged and watched." I finished my shake.

I stood and got a bottle of water from the fridge.

"Look who can move," Matt teased.

I stuck my tongue out at him as I opened my pharmacy bag. I read the directions and opened the bottle. Downing one pill and half the bottle of water, I hoped the drug would help the spider bite heal faster.

Ivy and Gunnar walked back in.

"Okay, I'm a genius." Ivy strutted around the kitchen. "Gunnar is adorable, and he needs to learn to mix drinks. I can't put together a training schedule until next week. But Gunnar was a cop. Police academy, right?" she asked.

Matt nodded. "So?"

"So, he can help De. Part assistant and part bodyguard. I'm going to get him your meds, and he'll make sure you take them. That you eat and always have water." Ivy gave Gunnar a look.

"You got it. No worries. I can handle anything. Even if she passes out." Gunnar gave me a thumbs up.

"I'm not exactly a size two." I would probably be up to a fourteen soon, considering how I'd eaten today.

He scooped me up and cradled me like the cover of an old romance novel.

"Strong enough, check." Ivy grinned. "I'll get the rest of the meds upstairs. Be right back. Gunnar, if she needs to be carried out of a situation, you bring her right back here. She can't solve a case that weak. You can drive her SUV so she can rest her eyes on the ride at least."

"Got it." He nodded and put me back down.

I was outvoted, and truthfully, I didn't feel up to driving, anyway. Ivy was a genius when she needed to be.

At first, just randomly driving around seemed silly. I gave Gunnar directions to stay heading one way over another. There was so much waterfront and bayou that there was nothing to do but go on gut feeling. I held the picture of the girls. We made it to a community on the water and finally had to park.

We got out of the SUV, and Gunnar was right there with a big bottle of water and granola bars in hand, plus a bag of meds.

Matt looked around. "Nearby or way out?"

I looked out over the water. "Houseboat or boat. On the water. We'll need a boat."

Matt nodded and got on his radio.

Back in my SUV, we followed Matt's car to a dock where a big airboat roared up.

I got the seat next to the pilot. "Point, and I'll follow," he said.

I nodded and closed my eyes.

As he took off, the noise and wind had a sensory deprivation effect, but I didn't need to hear. I needed to feel. The girls were alive but drugged and weak. There was another boat behind us with a few more police officers. The girls weren't alone, and the more I was in their head space, the more I understood. The man who had them was very bad. Very scary.

I pointed, again, and felt the boat gear down and putter to a stop.

I opened my eyes. We had five houseboats docked, but they were hard to see tucked in amongst thick brush and trees.

We were far enough away that no one had noticed us, hopefully. But all five structures looked the same. You'd never guess behind the walls of one of them was a dangerous kidnapper.

"None of them have boats parked out front," Gunnar said.

"Doesn't matter. That one. The girls are there." I pointed to the third house in the row.

The team of police decked out with riot gear went ahead. They tossed something into the window that smoked then the team of men rammed the door after a few minutes.

We climbed from the boats to the dock of the first houseboat while we waited for more information.

The lead cop stepped out. "Empty!" he called out to us.

"No!" I ran forward.

"The smoke..." Gunnar held me back.

"We're airing it out. But it looks like people were held here recently," the man reported to Matt as the pilot idled the airboat up alongside the floating house.

"We just missed them? Come on." I wanted to start today over, again. Nothing had gone right, at all.

Matt stepped off the boat, stuck his head in the now open door and waved us in.

I took it all in immediately. The big mattress on the floor was just as I'd seen it. "The girls were tied up there."

"We're going to have CSI come in. Check for DNA and prints. I've got officers going door to door nearby and see what people saw or heard." Matt looked around.

Gunnar shook his head. "Around here, no one sees a thing. Half these boats are probably empty. Used for fishing or gator baiting and killing."

"Gator killing." I shuddered.

"Relax. Try to get a feel for where they were moved. One of the girls may have gotten loose and found the kidnapper's cell phone. Or screamed for help. Do you think it's human trafficking?" Matt asked.

I closed my eyes and reached out for the girls. They were on the move. In the back of a van or SUV. They were terrified and had no idea what the plan was.

I tried to focus on the kidnapper. "He's not a rapist. He hasn't touched any of them. He's using them for something."

"Will they change hands soon?" Matt pushed.

I followed the girls in my head.

Suddenly, Gunnar grabbed me and scooped me up.

"What the...?" I opened my eyes.

We were at the edge of the boat dock.

"You almost walked into the water. Miss Ivy would kill me," he said.

"Sorry. They're traveling, right now. I think the guy is looking for a place to hold up and be safe until the news dies down. If they are looking to sell the girls or something like that, it won't happen while it's a hot issue." I looked at the ground. "You can put me down, now."

Gunnar carried me over to Matt on dry land and set me on my feet. Then, he handed me my bottle of water.

I drank without argument. But this wasn't the spider bite, it was just me. Getting into my visions and focusing on my work made me completely oblivious to my true surroundings.

"The team is moving in here. I need to take you back to the station for a statement and to decide what's next. The girls' mothers want to meet you, as well." Matt patted my arm.

"I'm not in a good state to meet people." I ran my fingers through my hair.

"You're the best hope for finding their kids. They want to meet you. It's not a judgment," Matt said.

"You don't understand women, at all." I shook my head at him.

"Let's get on the boat." Gunnar guided me like I was a blind girl.

Another half an hour drive to the police station, and I was ready to sleep for a week.

At first, we were in an office, and I gave Matt my statement. I tried to pin down where the girls were, but they were still in a van on the move.

A few minutes later, three women were led in.

Matt cleared his throat. I looked up, and Gunnar stood.

"This is Mrs. Richards, Ms. Loupe, and Ms. Duets. Their daughters are Kimmie, Julie, and Didi. This is Deanna Oscar. She's solved many cases for us and has already helped us find where the girls were being held," Matt said.

"Where are they, now?" Ms. Duets asked firmly.

"I think the girls must've tried to escape or something. The man who has them is relocating them. They're currently in a van." I understood the concern the mothers had. They were all desperate, but I felt a deep anxiety from Ms. Duets and Mrs. Richards.

"At least they're together and alive," Mrs. Richards said.

I understood what she meant. Julie was the only white girl among them. It was sad to say, but would the press cover it as heavily if all the girls were black? Especially in big cities, people got jaded with all of the violence and reports of crimes. Chicago was no different. As a regular person living your life, you could only care so much. I had some gifts that made all this my business. My problem.

"They are still together. They haven't been hurt that I can tell, beyond being drugged. I will try, again, once they've stopped moving."

"Why wait? Go out now and drive. Follow them!" Ms. Loupe said.

Matt stepped in. "We've got Amber Alerts out on the girls. We're taking samples from the place they were held to confirm. But a high-speed chase through traffic at rush hour isn't going to help the girls. The kidnapper could crash the van or drive off a bridge. If he panics, your girls could be dead."

"What's stopping him from killing them when he finds a new abandoned house to hold up in?" Ms. Duets asked.

"If he wanted them dead, they'd be dead by now. At least one of them. He's not violent. I wish I could give you more details, but the girls are groggy from the drugs." I shrugged.

"Did they go off with someone or did they think he was the Uber driver?" Mrs. Richards asked.

I closed my eyes and dug into their subconscious. Kimmie's drug-hazed mind seemed to be replaying the abduction in a constant feedback loop. She wasn't drugged to the point of unconsciousness, as if their abductor just wanted her compliant. Lucky for me, Kimmie was alert enough to share some information. The images were fuzzy but viable. "He pretended to be their Uber and then drove off to some remote road. Locked the doors and used chloroform to knock them out. They thought they were coming home." It was small comfort, but it was something.

"Girls are never safe in this world." Ms. Loupe wiped her tears away.

"I'll do everything I can. I'm sorry. It's been a bad day for me, so I'm not at full strength," I admitted.

Gunnar handed me some pills, and I took them.

"We appreciate your help. Anything you can do to get our girls back," Mrs. Richards said.

I nodded but felt like crap. I should be able to do this. The pressure wasn't even coming from the mothers. It was me. It was those scared young girls. Why would this man take them? I didn't get the sense he planned to sell them into sexual trafficking. Then again, he wasn't planning to be violent with them either. It made no sense. He wasn't personally interested in them. He had power and coveted power, but what could three teen girls do to help with that? He was working for someone else.

"You'll feel better after a good night's rest. Hit this fresh in the morning," Gunnar said.

I nodded. "I should go. Matt will keep you updated, I'm sure."

Gunnar guided me out. "You okay? You look blank," he said.

"I'm trying to figure out the bad guy," I said.

"You need to rest." He opened my car door.

I got inside. "Thank you, Gunnar. Not sure I'd have made it through today without you."

He smiled and started the car. "You'd have taken a bayou dip. Not good for the spider bite. All sorts of bacteria and crap in that water. Pace yourself. You'll get the bad guy and recover."

I hoped I could do both fast.

Chapter Five

The rest of the day was a blur of dinner, pills, and Gunnar giving Ivy and Greg a detailed rundown of the investigation. Ivy was impressed enough to hire Gunnar for the rest of the week to cart me around like I was helpless.

"I can drive. No one said I couldn't drive or do everything normally," I said as Ivy fussed.

"You close your eyes when you're getting visions. That's not good when you're driving. Gunnar is trained like a cop but has the body of a stripper. Plus good Southern manners. How can you object?" Ivy handed me the remote to the TV.

"Fine. But once I'm back to normal, I don't need a babysitter," I said.

"We'll see. You've always had someone along with you. If Greg is working a lot, you might need to hire an assistant. I'm too busy with the club, now. You have water, some cheese and cracker packets if you get hungry, and all your meds. But you should be good for the night." Ivy checked the nightstand.

"I'm so sick of pills," I said.

"Well, you can argue with the doctor over breakfast. He'll be here early, so you can try to have a normal day. You're welcome," Ivy said sarcastically.

"Thank you. I know I'm a terrible patient. I don't usually get sick." I still felt the dark cloud over me. The spider bite was part of it.

"The good news is you'll live. Sleep. Forget the case and about the bite. Just rest. Find some mindless sitcoms and think happy thoughts." Ivy opened the door, and Tish the cat darted for the bed.

"Don't let her lick your spider bite," Ivy said.

"Goodnight, Mom," I said.

Ivy left, and Tish immediately went to the wound and sniffed. She didn't lick it but cuddled up on the other side of my neck. I dozed with the white noise of the TV helping my mind not focus on anything.

But that only worked for so long. Deep sleep meant dreams. I was on the dirty mattress and tied up. I felt the girls' fear and helplessness. They only had liquor to drink, and he drugged them on top of it. He wasn't acting nice or mean to them; he was mechanical. Like a robot doing as programmed.

At night, they were cold and hungry. I saw them trying to find a way out. They weren't traveling, anymore, but the man had made sure they were far away from other people and surrounded by water. Even if the girls could swim, there were things in that water that could kill them. Poisonous snakes, spiders, and gators.

I tried to tell them to cooperate. To rest. They were safe, for now, and we would come and find them. But then, someone was after me, not them. He was a shadow, but I felt how real he was. A man out to kill me. He pulled a gun.

I sat up in bed, and poor Tish flopped on the mattress.

She meowed at me.

"Sorry. Bad dream." I scratched her ears as she curled up on the other pillow. She purred with forgiveness but fell asleep, again, fast.

"Two men I have to worry about?" I turned up the light just enough on my bedside lamp that I could focus on the room. "Death."

I didn't care if it was a cute guy, the Jamaican woman, or Bozo the Clown. I needed answers.

"Death," I summoned again softly. I'd never get answers if I woke up Ivy or Greg.

The same woman from earlier appeared. Her annoyed expression reflected how I felt.

"What do ya want, now?" Death asked.

Tish stood and hissed, her fur standing on end.

"Go on, Tish, go sleep downstairs." I shooed her out the door and closed it to avoid interruptions. "Sorry, I have to ask you a few questions."

"For someone not on de list, you're full of dem." She sat on the edge of my bed.

"So, I'm still not on your list?" I asked.

"No." She pulled out a scroll. "No. But it updates any time. Changes by de minute."

"Well, someone shot at me a few days back. Then, I got bit by a poisonous spider. Now, I'm having dreams that a man is out to kill me. A shadow man." I shook my head. "It doesn't make much sense."

"To me, it makes no sense. I'm just Death. I work de list. Your angel should help you," Death said.

My angel appeared, just then.

"Great. She never appeared to me until a few months ago. Seriously, I've seen dead people all my life and had visions. My own angel blocked me out. Why should I trust her?" I asked.

"Why should you trust me? You are not on de list. If you show up, I'll show up." Death shrugged then vanished.

"I liked the guy better." I crawled back under the covers.

"Your shadow man is no shadow," my angel announced.

"Good, have Death kill him before he kills me." I yawned.

"He is no joke either. You are being targeted. Do not let your guard down," she warned.

"Who is targeting me and why?" I asked.

"I can't tell you that," my angel replied.

"How helpful. So, someone is trying to kill me. A demon? A human?" I asked.

"Not a demon. More or less a human," she said.

"More or less," I said. "A ghost?"

"No, not a ghost. You'll understand in time. Don't drop your guard, no matter what the others tell you. Your friends can't protect you from this."

"Is it the same man who has these girls? I'm in danger when I'm working these cases. It happens. This feels different, not like a job." I shrugged and winced.

"It is not the same man. Both are dangerous in their own way. You need to rest. That bite is no joke either," she added.

"Really? Can I just ask why?" I sighed.

"Why?" She frowned at me. "Why what?"

"Why the spider bite? Why now? What purpose does this serve? The girls are scared, the moms are frantic, and I'm running at half strength because of a little brown spider. Seriously, wouldn't the big guy rather I help people faster?" I asked.

"I can't and don't ponder God's plan or timetable. People die before their natural life should be over every day. I don't question." She shook her head.

The glowing hair was getting on my nerves. Angels seemed backlit, somehow. "So, I have to bug God for answers? I don't feel up to astral projection."

"You shouldn't bug God. Trust and see how things unfold."

"I've had hard cases before. I can do that. But why the hell would I get dinged with a spider bite?" I asked.

"It's not a punishment. It's a reminder," she said.

"Reminder? Little bugs are as lethal as humans?" I asked.

"If that helps you. Also, a hint that you are human. You are subject to illness and infection. You must take care of yourself and balance your life."

"I thought I was doing okay. My brother's situation was one thing, but since then..." I trailed off.

"Since then, you got a new power you didn't even notice because you were barreling through doing things with Greg and helping others. New powers, new responsibility. Another thing for you to balance. So, you received a ticket to slow down a bit."

"A ticket from Heaven? Is there a fine or can I take a class?" I teased.

"Survive it and do your best. You must be challenged or you won't be able to handle what's coming," she said.

"Don't tell me that. I don't want to hear that. I don't feel any demons in this case. Just a bad guy doing bad things. Plus the bad guy after me. And the spider bite." I fell back on the pillows. "Thanks."

"You're welcome."

"Angels do not get sarcasm," I said.

"Please call me next time, at least at the same time, if you summon Death." She ruffled her wings.

"Are you going to tell on me that I called Death first? Or is it just your ego?" I taunted.

"Death far outranks me. If I can help, I should first," she said.

"You're always around. Show up. Death has a lot of other work to do, so I have to call him to me. You're supposed to be mine and looking out for me all the time."

"I am," she said.

"But you're limited to what you can do or tell me." I nodded. "Doesn't mean I'll stop asking."

"Asking for help is good. Getting angry at me is a waste of your energy. Rest. You'll need it." She vanished.

"Angels don't get any points for charm or people skills," I said out loud, and then, I remembered I'd put the cat out of the room. "Maybe I am crazy."

I took a long drink of water then buried myself under the covers. The case had nothing to do with the weird crap and the guy following me. But New Orleans was a big city, and some weirdo might get off on the idea of taking down a psychic police consultant.

The next morning, I managed to shower and dress before anyone started babying me. Ivy brought up eggs, bacon and toast as I was drying my hair.

She yanked the plug from the wall. "Sit, eat."

"Not done." I mimicked her order style and caveman talk. I plugged back in the dryer and finished my hair.

"You need to eat for your antibiotic," Ivy said as I hung up the dryer.

"I know. I also have a case to solve." I ignored the blister near my collarbone. It stung and ached, but there wasn't much I could do about it.

"You need to take care of yourself." She handed me a fork.

Ivy was dressed in a green paisley gown. She was clearly headed to the club. "I know. I can take care of myself. One little spider bite isn't worth all the fuss."

"That's ugly. The doctor should be here soon. Gunnar is on his way. He's your assistant until further notice. No arguments," she said.

I sat back. "I think you're forgetting who owns what around here. I know you're doing this because you care, but you're falling back into that boss mode. I know I was gone for a long time taking care of my brother. I appreciate all you did stepping up, and you run the club however you see as right. But my job is mine. I have to manage it, and sometimes, it can't wait.

I'm not going to do something stupid. I'm not going to be dictated to. I can fire you," I said.

"Fine. You pay Gunnar. When you're done with him, I'll transition him over to be a bartender. But your work is important. Those poor girls. Only you can do what you do. You need to hire a permanent assistant, I think. You try to act like it's nothing. It's normal. But you need the help. Greg and I might not be available, and you can't make Matt spare a uniform officer or something. You can afford it."

"This is normal for me." I hugged her. "I'm not that weird."

She laughed. "We're both weird. Now, eat. Personal assistants aren't weird, anyway. Rich people have them all the time."

"Fine. I'll give it serious thought. I need coffee." I sat and cleaned my plate.

Ivy went downstairs and came back with a huge glass of OJ and a big mug of coffee.

"Thank you." I downed the coffee.

I finished the food and was sipping the orange juice before I noticed the doctor loitering in the doorway.

"Come on in. I don't bite," I said.

"Are you feeling better?" he asked.

"This hurts more, but I'm less foggy and itchy." I grabbed my antibiotic and took it before anyone scolded me.

"Good. I've seen much worse allergic reactions to spider bites. Yours wasn't extreme, but the meds will make you sleepy and foggy. Keep up with the antibiotic, because this will open and can easily get infected. There will be some dead tissue to cut away." He touched around the blister.

"Ick," I said.

"Yep, but it's not spreading too much. So, hopefully, the damage will be minimal. Little scar." He smiled.

I stared at him.

"I'm sorry if I was weird the other day. I see dead people and angels. I saw the Angel of Death a while ago, and he looked just like you. I guess people who are near death or in comas... Some angels will borrow their forms." I shrugged.

"De, don't scare off the doc," Ivy said with a smile.

"No, it's fine. Weird, but that actually might explain some things. I was attacked in the ER some time back. Drug addict who came in strung out. He slipped the restraints and slammed my head into the wall. I was in a coma for a couple of weeks. They induced it, so the swelling in my brain could go down. I don't remember anything about when I was out." He listened to my chest.

"But you're all better? Right?" Ivy asked.

"Yes, I had to be fully checked out and tested before I was allowed to return to work. The brain is a remarkable organ. It can survive a lot," he said.

"I'm learning spiders are pretty powerful, too," I said.

He laughed. "Venom is very potent. We haven't studied all the unique uses and properties of venom in all the reptiles and spiders out there. But in their natural defense uses, they hurt like hell."

"What do I do with it?" I asked.

"Nothing. I'll monitor it daily. At some point, I'll need to cut some of the blistered flesh away. I'll make sure it won't hurt, but it will get uglier before it heals. Take your meds, lots of water, rest, and avoid bumping or scratching the blister." He nodded.

"Thanks," I said.

"Rest," Ivy said.

"I can go back to my normal work? If I'm careful? Right, Doc?" I asked.

"Sure. The worst is over with the allergic reaction. That's through your system, so you can stop the Benadryl. Just keep up with the other meds, and I'll see you tomorrow morning." He picked up his bag.

"Thanks, just send me a bill," I said.

"I wouldn't know what to charge for a house call," he chuckled.

"You'll figure it out. But I appreciate you coming here. I have to go to the police station," I said.

"Police?" He looked at me.

"I'm consulting on the missing girls case," I said.

"Good luck with that." He headed for the hallway and nearly collided with Gunnar.

"Sorry, Doc. Hey." Gunnar shook his hand.

"The stripper?" the doctor asked.

"I'm doing some odd jobs, now, too," Gunnar said.

"My work is very odd," I said.

"See you tomorrow." The doctor locked eyes with me but left.

Ivy and I laughed. Gunnar shook his head. "Why do people have to judge?"

"Humans are flawed beings." I grabbed my purse. "Let's get the meds, get some waters, and hit the road."

"You're the boss. You look a lot better today. It's in your eyes." Gunnar went to work collecting what we'd need to safely get going.

It was easy watching him work. I hadn't fully appreciated his form yesterday. I really had been sick.

Chapter Six

Gunnar went for the driver's side, and it felt weird for me to get in the passenger side of my own SUV.

"To the police station?" he asked.

I shook my head. "No, to the trailer park those three girls are from."

"Without the police?" he asked.

"The girls aren't there, now. We don't need the police. They have enough work to do. If I don't know where the bad guy is, then we don't need them. The cops are spread thin enough. I don't waste their time unless they can arrest someone. Ivy made a good choice with you. Cop training, but you're not on their payroll," I said.

"Are the three girls still being moved around?" he asked.

I shook my head. "I can't pinpoint them. Something is clouding my read."

"Maybe you should go home and rest for another day. You overworked yourself yesterday, and you looked like hell. You seem better today, but exhaustion is a killer. I've seen it. A day in bed might reset things," he suggested.

"How many psychics have you worked for?" I asked him.

"None, ma'am. But my mom worked two jobs, seven days a week. When she got sick, it really took it out of her because she ran herself ragged, never wanting to call off. I know those girls need your help, but if you can't nail down their location, admit it and take the day off," he said.

"They could be dead by tomorrow. Or handed off to someone buying them and taking them out of the country. It's too risky. If I get what I need to get done, then I'll rest this afternoon. But I can't hide at home for a whole day while they suffer. I won't get the rest you think I will. It's all connected to my brain, no matter where I am." I watched the mirror as Gunnar pulled into traffic.

"That is a sucky job. Cool powers but sucky when you need a day off," he said.

"No arguments here," I said.

It took a few minutes, but a beat-up old Cadillac pulled out and followed us.

I was a little paranoid. I kept one eye on the mirror and tried to relax and fixate on the girls. It seemed easy in my dream, but not now. Until things cleared up, I had to try and link up to the girls and shake my shadow man.

"I'm sure this isn't the job you were hoping for. Bartending is more fun. I'm sure stripping is more...something," I said.

He laughed. "I haven't tended bar before, but that'll be nice. Stripping is good money. The police training helped me handle any bad situations I ran into. When you grow up poor, making money is hard. The only easy ways are illegal. I didn't want to do that."

"Sell drugs, you mean," I said.

He smirked. "Or sell something else. My dad was into drugs and bailed on us. My mom was strict about that stuff." Gunnar kept his eyes on the road.

"Oh. I'm glad you found stripping, then. I guess. This is probably boring," I said.

"Nah. I liked police work. I wanted to make detective, but even then, the pay wasn't great, and the work was dangerous. My mom worried. Stripping let me move her and my grandma to a nicer place. They have to share the house, but it's in a decent area, and Mom can cover the other expenses as long as I pay the rent. Grandma wanted a garden, and now, she has it. No more apartments for them." He pulled into the trailer park.

I looked back at the Cadillac still following us.

"That's very nice of you," I said.

He smiled. "I'll do this as long as you want me to. I like helping the police without the politics and rank crap."

"Did they pick on you because you were gay?" I asked.

"Nah, I was made a gay liaison officer. I had a rainbow on my uniform and everything. For real. It was small, right over my badge, but it helped gays not freak if I approached, ya know? But I didn't always fit in with the other guys. Their girlfriends or boyfriends would flirt with me if I went out with friends after work. I didn't flirt, but it gets weird. And I wasn't good at being hard on people. Never gave out enough tickets and such. Too many warnings." He shrugged.

"You're too nice," I said.

He nodded. "Matt talked to me once about it. Said maybe I should try parole officer or working in the juvie system. None of the money could match what I make at night. I can work for you during the day and strip at night. I do private parties, not clubs. So, it's all good."

"And Ivy?" I asked.

"I don't want to let her down. Whatever you two want. Bartending was never a goal in my life, but I won't be this young and pretty forever. It'd help with the tips." He laughed. "I'm joking."

"Right. How young are you?"

"Twenty-six. I know, I look younger." He brushed his longer bangs out of his face, and those piercing blue eyes were magical. He was a sweet guy who knew how to use his gifts.

"You do look younger. You want to assist a sometimes-grouchy psychic?" I asked.

"Who solves crime and helps people? Why not?" He hopped out of the SUV.

I examined the trailer park, and my heart sank.

Gunnar opened my door like a gentleman. "What's wrong?"

"This is depressing," I said softly.

There was little space between the trailers, and most looked rundown.

"Yeah. You're not in the Garden District, anymore, Dorothy," he said.

64

"Are these FEMA trailers?" I asked.

"Some might be. Don't worry; you're safe with me." Gunnar closed the door after I stepped out and locked it.

"It's not that. I just feel...that I hate this world, sometimes," I said.

"I get that. You learn to wall off that part of your brain being a cop. You want to help everyone, but you can't make them make different choices. Some people won't take help or advice. Do you want to talk to the girls' families?" he asked.

I shook my head. "I just need to walk around a bit and feel."

"You got it. Walk. Close your eyes. I've got your back...or front."

I giggled. I wasn't one to giggle, but Gunnar had a way of phrasing things.

"Only as appropriate and for safety's sake," he clarified.

"I'm a straight psychic woman who owns a drag club—it's really hard to offend me." I closed my eyes for a moment and just felt for the girls.

They lived close to each other. Two of the families were struggling every bit as much as the neighborhood indicated. Another one had more money in the bank, but they were living below their means. I couldn't argue with it. People had overdone it on houses and then paid a steep price when the market corrected. Living simpler was smarter, but her friends didn't know she had any more.

"What are you feeling for?" Gunnar asked.

I held up a finger. I glanced around and spotted my stalker. Was he a demon or something else? A demon I could sense. This guy was like a shadow. I felt nothing, but he was following me.

"I'm trying to feel if anyone here had been watching the girls. If they were targeted by someone they knew. I don't think they know their kidnapper, but maybe he knew them." I turned around in order to pull from all directions.

"And?" he asked.

"I don't think they were watched or picked out by anyone here. There are a few pervs who like looking at teenage girls that live in this park, but they weren't involved." I shuddered.

"Cold?" he asked.

"Grossed out. Some men are sick." I took a deep breath.

"Don't I know it. I've stripped for men and women. I prefer women for an audience." Gunner handed over a bottle of water.

"Thanks." I took a long drink and spotted my stalker. "I think someone is following me."

"Navy blue Caddy? Yeah, I've got an eye on him," Gunnar said.

My face must've given away my shock.

"I was top of my class at the police academy. I didn't want to scare you, but you were sort of watching him, too. I thought maybe you were having me watched. So, that guy is not our friend?" Gunnar asked.

"I can't read him. No, he's not our friend. I had bad dreams about a shadow man stalking me."

"You're the psychic. Want me to go shake him up?" Gunnar asked.

"No. I got what I need from here. Let's swing by The Third Eye. Some friends own it, and I want to see if he'll follow us in a small store. And see what they think of him. Can you get a picture of him?" I asked.

"Sure. I'll pretend I'm taking one of you. Wave like we're taking a video so I can get a few shots and zoom in." Gunnar pulled out a new big cell phone.

I waved and blew kisses at the phone and said "hi" and other random stuff like I was making a video to send to my mom.

"Good. Got it. Let's go before he gets too close or paranoid." Gunnar unlocked the car and opened the door for me.

"Thanks." I sat and closed my eyes.

Gunnar drove through the trailer park and out the back.

"Have you been here before?" I asked.

"Not this one, but I grew up in a park like this. They always have a back way out. Want lunch? We can see if the guy follows us for sandwiches," he said.

I shook my head. "The Third Eye first. Then lunch."

"You're the boss," he said.

Gunnar found a spot in the crazy and crowded area just off the French Quarter. The Third Eye was a bit of everything New Age shop. Faith and her mom, Myrna, were the owners. They were witches, but I didn't judge.

The Caddy went on around to circle for a spot. We went inside like we didn't suspect a thing.

Faith brightened up a lot when she saw Gunnar.

"Hi, Deanna, who's your friend?" she asked.

"This is Gunnar. Gunnar, this is Faith. Is your mom around?" I asked.

She nodded. "Mom, come out please; it's Deanna."

Myrna appeared from the back and began to wave at the air around me. "Oh my, dear. You've got something on you."

"I got bit by a brown recluse." I pointed to my neck.

"No. Not that. Although, it might be part of it. You've got a curse on you," Myrna said.

"A curse?" I laughed.

"Don't mock. Curses are real. They can do harm," Faith said.

"Like a demon cursed her?" Gunnar asked.

"No, not a demon. A human. It's of this world."

"Can you get rid of it?" I asked.

Myrna shook her head. "It's not my magic. You need to find the source. But we can help."

"Help me with this stalker," I said.

Faith stared at the door.

"Show me some crystals," Gunnar said to Faith, and they went to browse.

"The demon was vanquished, but you made some enemies, it seems," Myrna said softly.

The bell over the door jingled.

"Can I help you, sir?" Myrna addressed the man who'd been following me.

I didn't turn around and pretended to be looking at some of the jewelry in the front case.

"I'm just looking for some incense," he said rather sluggishly.

Maybe he was a fan of the show I was featured in? Ghost Tamers had aired recently. Maybe he was mentally challenged in some way, and I'd missed it. Or his mind was wired a bit differently, so it was hard for me to read. He might be a stalker fan who didn't know how to handle it. I wanted to give him the benefit of the doubt. I really didn't want to believe I had a stalker out to kill me. Not that this explained the shooting at my club.

"Right corner. Back of the store." Myrna waved him in the right direction.

The man was staring at me. I looked up and caught his eye, and he looked away briefly. The moment that I turned my head, he just kept staring. I felt his eyes on my every move.

Gunnar walked over, and the guy rounded the incense to the candles to keep a distance between them. He was also trying to keep an eye on me and managed to bump the table.

The lit candle wobbled in its loose holder then fell and ignited a nearby tapestry on the densely decorated table.

"Fire!" I shouted. I looked around for something to put out the flames, but the whole place was a tinder box. Plenty of candles, incense, and dried herbs. The scarf display was too close. Many of the cases and tables were solid wood. The fire spread over the small table quickly, the tablecloth and all the pretty decorations glowing an eerie, hellish red.

Gunnar tossed a scarf or two on it, but the flames were too high to be smothered by something so thin. The smoke detectors began to blare. I waited for the sprinklers to go off.

I looked up, as did Gunnar.

"Sprinklers?" I asked.

"Old building. This is the historic district. No sprinkler system," Myrna said.

The panic level went up, and I pulled out my phone to call 911.

"Wait, De. Mom, where did you move the fire extinguisher?" Faith was under the counter, frantically tossing out boxes and bags of things.

"It's in the back," Myrna shouted.

Faith ran to the back and brought out a fire extinguisher. On the verge of tears, she fumbled with the key. Gunnar grabbed the big red canister and handled it like a pro. He put out the fire and coated the area around the table to catch any jumping embers.

When the powder and smoke cleared, the creepy man was gone.

"Check the back. Make sure he's not hiding in here," Myrna ordered.

Gunnar and Faith went through every back room and every aisle.

"Gone." Faith shook her head.

"We've got him on security camera footage." Myrna pointed at the cameras in the ceilings.

"Thanks, but we have a picture of him. We just don't know who he is," I said.

Gunnar showed them the zoomed-in pic.

"He's got those creepy eyes." Faith shook her head.

"I wish he were a demon. I could sense a demon." I shrugged.

"No, he's not that powerful. He's a human, but he might be..." Myrna tucked her hand under her chin and her ten bracelets jingled.

"A what?" I asked.

"A zombie. He was focused on you. He barely noticed Gunnar until he spoke. He knocked over a candle and barely paid attention to the fire." Myrna nodded. "He's programmed."

"Like a cult?" I asked.

"Brainwashing is a big part of making a zombie, but the rest? That's Haitian Voodoo." Myrna pulled a card from under the counter. "This place has practitioners who might be able to give you more information. I don't know anyone who makes zombies, but that's big power."

"Is this also where the curse came from?" Faith asked.

"Probably," Myrna confirmed. "You've landed on someone's radar or pissed off someone you'd rather not have angry with you. They are not minor league or playing with white magics."

"Who are they? Any ideas?" I asked.

"It won't be easy to pinpoint them. Many people play with the dark arts at home. They'll be hiding in the shadows and blocking your powers as much as possible. The curse could bring bad luck, bad dreams, interference with your powers. All designed to weaken you so the zombie can do its job." Myrna sighed.

"What job exactly?" Gunnar asked.

"Whatever job its master gave him. Kidnapping or killing, most likely. Maybe get hair or something for another spell. But they probably already have something of yours since they set the curse on you." Myrna shook her head. "Consult the Voodoo specialists. You'll need their help to break the spell or track the zombie master."

"Will they talk to me?" I asked.

"As long as you're respectful, they will. I'll call Tamara and tell her to expect you." Myrna made herself a note.

"So, these zombies don't want brains? They just do as they're told?" Gunnar asked.

"This isn't The Walking Dead. This is real. He can and will complete his orders. No matter what you do to him or put in his way. He has only one goal, right now. Hurting him or making him immobile are the only ways to give yourself some breathing room," Myrna said.

"Great. And this spider bite had me feeling like a zombie yesterday. He's ahead of us," I said.

"It's hard to tell how long he's been on the job watching you. But I'd stay close to home or protection until you can get to the Voodoo shop. They'll help." Myrna patted my hand.

"Thanks. I guess I better go home and rest up. Between spiders and missing girls, I have to be on my game tomorrow," I said.

"If we can help, let us know," Faith offered.

"Thanks. You should call the police and the fire department. Report the incident, since the customer set a display on fire. Plus, you'll need a report for your insurance." I nodded to Gunnar, and he opened the door for me.

I could get used to a sweet and hot Southern guy opening doors for me all the time.

Chapter Seven

Gunnar made us drive through for lunch so we could take it home. We ate at my kitchen table.

"I'm not exhausted. I'm fine," I said.

"It's not just about you, now. You're a target. We can lock up the house. If he steps on your property, we call the cops," Gunnar said.

"You're right." I set my sandwich down. "I need to do something quick."

Gunnar nodded.

I walked into the living room and lit two tall candles next to the urn with Gran's ashes.

"Amy. Angel Amy," I said.

She appeared.

"A zombie?" I asked.

She didn't respond.

"A curse?" I asked.

"I can't change it or remove it," she said.

"But you can protect this property. Keep that guy off my land. I don't want the animals or anyone else hurt. He's after me, fine. Can you do that? Arrange it?" I asked.

"Angels don't do your bidding," she said.

"Fine, then don't get mad when I don't ask you for help. Gran!" I called.

"You think ghosts can help you?" the angel asked.

"Missy! Noah!" I called.

Missy and Gran showed up. Missy was a former maid who died in the late 1890s—who had chosen not to cross over. I'd never gotten the story as to why she preferred to work in my house rather than face her judgement, but since my own brother had tried the same stunt, I wasn't about to judge. Luckily, my late brother had crossed over and faced his reality. Heaven was a lot nicer than my kitchen.

Noah never showed himself. He generally kept to the library. He never really talked either. He communicated through sounds and books. He was no demon; he was good—I could tell that much. But why he chose to stay or if he was related to me, I had no idea. Somehow, I did feel better with him around the house. He kept an eye on things. A house with bad spirits locked in the attic and possessed objects stored under the stairs needed a watchdog.

"What's wrong, dear?" Gran asked.

"Good question. Someone has cursed me. I guess angel protection isn't perfect. There's also a zombie after me. He has been stalking me. Gunnar saw him. I'll touch base with a Voodoo contact tomorrow to see how to deal with it. But I want the house to be safe. To be protected. I don't want Ivy or Greg or the animals hurt. I want to be able to sleep. At the very least, I want to be alerted if the zombie steps one toe on my property. Noah and Missy are pretty good at that, but they might need some extra help, Gran," I said.

"I'll sit watch while you sleep," Gran said.

I smiled. "Thanks, but if you can keep watch of the house from up there, that's good enough for me. Alert Missy or Noah if you see anything, and they can take action."

Noah made two snapping sounds that indicated he agreed. I wish I could see him. My mysterious ghost seemed content to exist. Missy cooked and cleaned, just as she had in life, as a maid employed in the house long before I moved in.

Missy nodded. "We'll be ready."

"Thank you. I guess angels are pacifists," I said.

Amy stood straighter. "Angels are warriors. Read your Bible."

"Honey, I went to Catholic school. I remember well enough. But you're not helping, so I'll have to make due with a ghost army. Thank you." I headed back to the kitchen.

Gunnar sat down like he hadn't been listening in.

"You really have ghosts guarding the house?" he asked.

"I do, now. There are always ghosts here, but now, they know what's going on. You can leave. I'm just going to rest and see what I can feel." I filled a water bottle then tossed away the trash from lunch.

"Maybe I should stay?" he asked.

"Why? I can make it up the stairs just fine. See if Ivy needs help. I'm fine today. Tomorrow, I'll be busy, again. You wanted me to take today off. Well, half a day is still rest," I said.

"Fine. Tomorrow, the Voodoo shop?" he asked.

"Probably. Maybe the case, too. I have to call Matt and get an update on things." I checked my phone. "And charge my phone while I take a nap."

Gunnar nodded. "Lock the door behind me."

"I will. Be careful that zombie doesn't stalk you to eliminate an obstacle to me," I said.

I locked the door behind him and headed upstairs. Missy was watching out the front windows. The back was a maze of lush gardens. Everything back there was locked up tight. Trudging up the stairs, I wanted my energy back.

I flopped on the bed and remembered my phone. Time to test the new power. I focused on my phone and levitated it to the nightstand. The cord was there. I tried once to plug the phone in and missed.

It fell to the nightstand. I nearly got up and did it manually, but new powers weren't useful if I didn't master them.

I relaxed and tried again. The phone pinged to tell me it was charging. I set it on the nightstand gently. The water bottle was still pretty heavy, so I set that down manually. I took an antibiotic then kicked off my shoes.

The plan was a nap, but I couldn't put this off. I used my burgeoning mental abilities to dial Matt and put the phone on speaker.

"Hey, spider lady. How's the neck?" Matt asked.

"A big icky blister. How's the case?" I asked.

"We followed up on all of the Amber Alert calls, but so far, nothing. We've got all the beat cops looking out for suspicious vans, but that doesn't narrow it down. Do you have them?" he asked.

"I'm messed up, Matt. I'm cursed or something. I've got a freaking zombie after me," I admitted. I sounded crazy to anyone who didn't live in my slice of reality.

"Zombie? Curses? Welcome to New Orleans. Who'd you piss off?" he asked.

"Plenty of people since I've been working with you. I have to go to this Voodoo person tomorrow to consult with on how to get rid of this crap," I said.

"The moms want you on the case. They were frustrated, but they are desperate."

"Flattering. I wasn't much help on my first day. I thought they might want me off the case," I said.

"They'll kiss your feet if you bring back their kids alive. They're upset, now, and it gets worse by the day," Matt shot back.

"It's not my ego. I can't make my powers focus properly, right now." If I couldn't trust my powers, I could lead them on a wild goose chase. "If this guy is smart, he'll relocate them every few days, just in case people are paying attention. Hell, he'll move them out of state as soon as he can."

"I told them that. I explained how human trafficking works. They'll try to get them far away very soon. Probably to Texas, then into Mexico before the Trump wall goes up. Damn, we'll probably see a surge of crap across the borders. Anyway, we're keeping an extra eye on the borders and waterways. I'm not lying. Without you, I'm not hopeful," Matt said.

"I can try, but what if I'm wrong? You're wasting all that police time and effort then for nothing," I said.

"Sleep. See the Voodoo people in the morning. I'll meet you after lunch. They want you to see the girls' rooms. See if you connect to them more that way. If you're not too exhausted, it's worth a shot," Matt said.

"Sounds good. But I went by the trailer park this morning to feel it out. I don't think the kidnapper was watching them there or was from that area," I said.

"Nah, we've run everyone there. Checked alibis and backgrounds. You're right as far as that." He chuckled.

"I guess that's good. Okay. See you after lunch at the trailer park tomorrow," I said.

"Bringing your boy toy?" he asked.

"My assistant? Yes, probably. He's gay, so really, he's the perfect babysitter. I'm going to get some rest. See you tomorrow."

"Okay, spider lady. Take all the pills," he said.

"Bye."

I was allowed to come down for breakfast the next day, so I had to be looking better.

Ivy was in a purple cocktail dress. Greg had decided to make French toast and bacon.

"So, you rested all afternoon?" Ivy asked.

"Except for talking to Matt a little, yes. I want to get this crappy feeling behind me. This blister has to heal and be looked after, but I'm sick of feeling tired and foggy," I said.

"Feel better today?" Greg asked.

"Mostly. But I know the antibiotics are only part of it." I poured myself a second cup of coffee.

The doorbell rang. I froze for a second, worried it was my new stalker. I'd already told Greg and Ivy about my obsessed new friend, so it wasn't a shock when Ivy took charge and got to her feet after seeing my face.

Ivy walked to the door. "It's the doc."

I was relieved.

"Feeling better?" he asked.

"Yes, but the antibiotics are still making me a bit sleepy," I said.

Dr. Brimlow nodded. "Take them all. You'll see." He removed the bandage from my collarbone.

The expression on Ivy's face told me not to look.

"I'm going to numb the area and cut away the dead pieces so the rest can heal."

"I'm going to just eat in the dining room," Ivy said.

Greg smiled.

"So, this stalker—zombie or demon? Come on. You're on their radar," Greg said.

"Demons?" the doc asked.

"Spiders are the least of my problems. I have really weird work, sometimes," I said.

"Demons can make people think and do just about anything. They use the weak and damaged," Greg explained.

"I agree this zombie guy is probably weak and damaged. He was brainwashed and programmed, but whoever did that, I don't think they are weak. They put some curse or something on me. Probably caused the spider bite. I'm going to the Voodoo shop this morning to see if they can help untangle this." I knew

Greg might fight the idea of running to another religion.

"If they can help, great. Their practices were probably used to create it. That's no doubt the best way to destroy what they did." Greg poured me more coffee.

"I didn't expect you to say that. I know you respect other faiths, but even with a pretty strong demon, you managed to overpower it."

"We did," Greg corrected. "But a demon is a demon. We don't know about the other rituals. Could we overpower the result? Sure. But will that lift the underlying curse? I don't know. It could cause other unforeseen side effects. It'd take a lot of trial and error and focus. You won't do that. You're too busy with those girls."

"You're right. I don't have time to play games. Someone did something to me. It can be undone, so let's get it undone." I sighed when the doc finally put a fresh bandage on my neck.

"Who would want to do something bad to you?" he asked.

"You'd be surprised. My powers attract crazies when I'm just trying to help people," I said.

The doorbell rang, and Ivy opened it. Gunnar strolled in with confidence in his usual jeans, t-shirt and sunglasses.

"Ready for the Voodoo shop?" he asked.

"Almost. Sit down and have some breakfast," I said.

"Nah, I had a protein shake after the gym. But thanks, anyway. Smells great." He leaned on the fridge, out of the way of the kitchen traffic.

"Is the zombie man outside?" Ivy asked.

Gunnar nodded. "Yep, looks like he slept there. We could have him arrested, I suppose.

Rich neighborhood and all. Sleeping in his car is pretty much loitering."

"No, he'd get a ticket or something stupid. We want him gone," Ivy said.

"Not dead," I added.

"No, but deprogrammed and not trying to hurt you. Gone, living his life like he should be," Ivy said.

"Amen," Greg said.

"You going back to the bug house?" I asked him.

Greg nodded. "One more time. The teen is making it happen, so I need to talk with him. He could use a therapist, but the family is in need."

"I could make a referral," I said.

"I'll let you know how it goes." Greg put the dishes in the dishwasher.

"Well, I'm done. See you, again, tomorrow." The doc closed up his bag. "Water, antibiotics, a good night's sleep, and don't scratch or bump the affected area."

"Got it." I nodded.

Gunnar grabbed water from the fridge and my pills. "On it."

I finished off my bacon then wiped my hands. "Better go."

"Voodoo starts early?" Greg asked with a smirk.

"I want to run the zombie around to get him confused first. I don't want him charging us in the Voodoo shop. The guy is determined, but he's not that quick." I grabbed my purse and made sure I had everything. Then, I stood and joined Gunnar at the door. "Stay out of trouble, you guys."

Ivy fed bacon to little Pearl. "You're the one with the weirdo stalker. I've got the new mirror being delivered today. It has to be perfect. The glass men took days to get the front window repaired."

"I thought it'd take longer than that," I admitted.

"I have a way with men." Ivy smirked.

"And a very big umbrella policy with a quality insurer on the club. We better get our money's worth. Later," I said.

Greg waved, and Ivy waggled Pearl's tiny Chihuahua paw.

I shut the front door behind us, and Gunnar laughed.

"The dog thing is a little weird, right?" I asked.

"She needs a man," Gunnar agreed.

I spotted my stalker. He tried not to react but sat up a bit straighter in his vehicle.

Chapter Eight

Gunnar was certainly a local boy of the bayou. He'd taken the zombie on a car chase that would impress the cops. Of course, he had been a cop so he'd know these streets even better than most natives. I kept forgetting that. We'd practically shaken the zombie when Gunnar parked in front of the Voodoo shop.

"You're not in a hurry," Gunnar said when I didn't exit the car as quickly as I normally would.

"I just don't like the idea of giving another religion any power over me," I said.

"Power? Everyone has some power over everyone else. And it can be used for good or for bad. Myrna said this lady was good. Might as well go in and see what Priestess Tamara has to say." He opened his door.

Lazy or reluctant, I let him round the car and open my door.

I took a bottle of water with me. Once my feet hit the ground, I was determined. I entered the shop, and a young man gave me the eye.

Not the good eye. Not quite the evil eye, but he was skeptical.

"I don't think you're in the right place. This is not a tourist shop," he said.

"I'm not a tourist. I'm Deanna Oscar. Myrna gave me this card and said she'd call ahead." I slid the card on the counter.

Gunnar strolled around, looking.

The young man glanced at the card and nodded. "I'll be right back. Don't touch anything."

"That is so cool!" Gunnar pointed to a skull with a cigar in its mouth and wearing a top hat.

"Don't touch it. Looks like an altar," I said.

"That is loa Baron Samedi. God of Death. But you're not here about death," said a woman with a deep voice.

I turned to find her in jeans and a sweater, her hair tucked in a turban with some braids peeking out. Very modern and stylish. "I'm Deanna Oscar. I hope it's a good time."

She shook my hand. "No time is a good time to have a zombie after you or such a curse on your life. Myrna said she felt a curse. I feel this, too. Sit."

She waved me around to behind the counter. I sat in the chair. She lit a few candles and murmured words I couldn't make out. Tamara put her hand over my head and then down my sides as if feeling out my energy.

"You're a woman of great power. You use it to help others, and some would take advantage of that." She shook her head. "The curse was done by someone you know. But not alone. They had help."

"The zombie?" Gunnar asked.

"Shh," she replied to him.

"Can you undo the curse?" I asked.

She shook her head. "Only with the items used to perform the curse could I release it. The one who cast it did not use Voodoo. Not pure Voodoo."

"I thought that's how you made a zombie. Haitian Voodoo?" I asked.

"The zombie, yes. The curse is deeper. Darker. I will reflect on it and see if I can find the path to the heart of the evil caster. But they may be after your power, your money, or your life. Or all three. Voodoo can be used for good or evil, but this residue of the curse is pure evil for the power of it." She shuddered.

"So, we're just going to wait until you figure it out?" Gunnar asked.

Tamara shook her head. "Certainly not. I can counter some of the magic and give you protection."

"I'm not sure that's a good idea," I said.

"Because?" Tamara prompted.

"I don't practice Voodoo. Will any of that work on me?" I asked.

"It doesn't need to work on you. It only needs to work on your zombie. Do you have a picture of him?" she asked.

Gunnar showed her the picture of the zombie from his cell phone.

She stared at it intently for a few minutes.

"Thank you. Give me a few minutes," she said.

Tamara went into the back, again, and I looked around the shop. Gunnar gave me a shrug, as if to say he was along for the ride, but we weren't sure where we were going.

There were the usual incense and candles, which felt soothing, but I wasn't sure how this woman would help if the guy who cursed me wasn't even using pure Voodoo. I stared at the Catholic-related statues of Mary and Jesus. No doubt this place had some Santeria practitioners, as well. The saint statues were lined up like little soldiers.

Tamara returned with a small doll. It wasn't like the ones tourists bought with pins in it and decorated with symbols. It was more plain and simple.

"Voodoo doll?" Gunnar asked.

"Yes, it will protect you from the zombie," she said.

"How?" I asked.

"Maybe you provide the pins?" Gunnar suggested.

Tamara gave him a scolding look. "You can use pins. But odds are you don't want to kill the man."

"No, just unzombie him, if that's even a word," I said.

"Freeing a zombie is hard. He must exert his own free will or the master must release him. Death can break the bond. Also, a large trauma may free his mind. People who use pins go for the eyes or the heart. If you need to kill him, if it gets that dangerous, a pin to the heart will do it. Or a total twist of his neck. Of course, this would all be in self-defense. But if you're being pursued, a twist of the leg can be very effective. Breaking both is legs should ensure you're safe for a while," she said.

Gunnar held up a finger. "Can't the master guy just send another zombie?"

Tamara sighed. "He can if he has them ready made, but I doubt he has an army. Zombies are hard to make. They take a lot of time, effort, and energy. The master's will to control must be stronger than the zombie's free will. If he has another, get a picture, and we'll create another doll. But odds are, this is his only one. He may be trying to create others, but they often fail."

"So, he's not a dead guy?" I asked.

"Oh, no. The zombie is alive. His family may believe he died. Drug addicts are a popular prey for those looking to create zombies. Ply them with just enough drugs to keep them from feeling sick, and make them do your bidding to get any little bump of the drug. Take away everything they have, and you own them. The drug does, really, but it takes away some of the work. But I wouldn't consider that a pure zombie."

"Sounds like a pimp," Gunnar said.

"That, too. Though most hookers I've met had a drug problem before. We do an outreach at some of the shelters to help people fight their demons. A person who has given up control of their life to a drug won't object nearly as much to giving up their power to another person as long as they get that drug. But it's all speculation. Your zombie doesn't seem strung out. Then again, it's only one picture," she said.

"Thank you." I carefully took the doll.

"It's okay; you can keep it in your purse. It only harms the person if that is your intention. If it gets accidentally poked by a pen, nothing happens to the target," she said.

"It works for me even if I don't believe in Voodoo?" I asked.

"It doesn't matter if you believe—the zombie is the one subject to the doll. Subject to the powers of Voodoo. He's already given himself up to that power. You just have to believe that my powers work on Voodoo followers," she said.

"Thanks, again. What do I owe you?" I asked.

"Nothing. You do good for the community." She waved me off.

"But I have to pay for the doll," I said.

"Find those girls. That's all the payment I need," she said.

"You know about that? I don't know if I can. The curse is blurring my powers. Blocking my mind." I shrugged.

"You can do it. You'll find ways to work around and overcome it all," she said.

"Thanks." I headed for the door with more questions than when I'd entered.

Lunch boosted my energy but not my morale. It was harder to exit the car at the trailer park than it had been at the Voodoo shop. This time, I knew the moms were there waiting for me. Hoping I'd get a hit off their teens' rooms. Few people really understood how psychic impressions happened. They varied by case and situation.

"You look better," Matt said.

"Thanks. I don't have a solid read on them. These mothers are going to be disappointed," I said.

"You're not at your best, now. Under the weather with a spider bite. I get it. Do your best. The worst scenario is when parents feel like we're doing nothing," Matt said.

"So, it's just for show?" I asked.

"All we got from the last scene was the girls' DNA. Proof they were there. Nothing on anyone else. This guy is good. Hope is fading," Matt said.

"Okay, I'll try." I followed him into a trailer.

"Kimmie loved school. She didn't have a lot of other talents, but she studied and swore she'd get a scholarship. Full ride. She'll be so mad about missing this much school," Mrs. Richards said through the sniffles. She wore purple scrubs with hearts and supportive shoes like she worked in a hospital. The color looked good against her dark skin. Her large eyes swam with tears, and she had a scarf over her head as though she couldn't handle doing her hair. I couldn't blame her. We were standing in her missing teenager's bedroom.

"I understand. Can I get a moment alone?" I asked.

She nodded, and Matt closed the door as he ushered the mom out.

The tiny room was a cheerful mix of blue and purple, both bright. When did neon come back in fashion? Squeezing between the twin bed and the desk, I could feel her struggle to work hard and not be discouraged. I could feel her drive.

I tried to reach out. The girl was alive and fighting.

I picked up a blue ribbon from her nightstand and walked out.

"Anything?" Mrs. Whatever asked.

"She's alive still. She's strong. Can I hold onto this?" I asked.

She nodded.

Matt cleared his throat. "Let's visit all the girls' homes and see where we are."

I followed him, glad of the fresh air, leaving one home. But the next was just as depressing.

Small and sparsely furnished with secondhand stuff. I was going to give my dad less crap the next time we talked. I wasn't supported much as a kid with special powers, but I had a nice home and whatever I needed. I couldn't keep up with a trashy celebrity family, then, but I did keep up with my middle-class classmates.

"Her mom isn't up to talking, but she said go ahead and take a look around." Matt led me from the front step to Julie's bedroom and closed the door behind me.

I walked the room. She was a cheerleader and a girly girl. There were posters on her walls and hot pink duct tape on her sneakers.

I found a pink ponytail holder and pocketed it. The mother wouldn't mind and having a better connection than a picture might just help. I mentally tried to reach the girl, but she was in a state of fear and shock. No pain, but she felt paralyzed.

Exiting that room, I heard the mom softly weeping. It fueled my determination, but raw fury couldn't force anything.

One more trailer to go. Gunnar handed me a water, and I paused to drink.

"Next one is a double wide. That's better," he said.

"Okay." I gave him back the bottle and followed Matt.

"This mother is working, right now, but she left me the key. She really wants your help and her daughter back. Gotta respect her for going to work," he said.

"Sitting around isn't helping anyone." I marched up the stairs.

This one was more open. More normal and less of that in-line feeling of a trailer. Gunnar knew his mobile homes. I found the girl's bedroom. She had more stuff; it wasn't expensive or fancy, but she had more. More shoes on the floor and clothes in her closet. I found a hair clip and pocketed it. She had a jewelry box full of earrings and bracelets.

With all three items in my pocket, I tried to feel the direction they were in. But my mind flashed on numbers, instead.

I started to repeat a string of nonsense numbers.

I opened the bedroom door, and Matt stared at me as I said the numbers over and over.

He finally grabbed his pad and scribbled them down.

These were the moments when I knew I could be committed. I was somewhere in between reality and touching some higher knowledge. Matt escorted me down the hall and toward the front door as I inhaled deeply, breathing in despair and grief along with this morning's burnt toast.

I felt crowded and wanted fresh air. Sure, I could fit the entire trailer in my dining room, but I hadn't been raised that way. I wasn't spoiled, but I was feeling a bit claustrophobic. Finally, I made it down the steps. Matt fumbled with the front lock as I repeated the sequence and enjoyed the fresh air and sunshine. The overall trailer park was still depressing, but I wasn't feeling trapped any longer.

"She got the Tourette's or OCD?" Gunnar asked.

"No, I don't know, but those numbers mean something," I said.

"Yeah, that's longitude and latitude. It means a dot on the map." Gunnar shrugged.

Matt grabbed a well-worn map of the New Orleans area from his car.

Spreading it on the hood of my SUV, he started to plot the point.

"You're sure they're there?" he asked.

"They are or were. I'm not trusting my accuracy, right now. Don't get the mothers' hopes up," I said.

Matt nodded. "We'll drive out and look around. No big fuss. You got a gun, junior?"

Gunnar frowned. "Not on me. I only usually take them when I do private stripping sessions."

"I'll loan you one, just in case. Good to have backup." Matt nodded.

"You can call a squad for backup. I just don't want to bring in the SWAT team when we're not sure if they're still there," I said.

Matt pointed to the map. "It's another houseboat. Down there, squads get noticed. Less is more."

We headed off to the bayou.

On the drive, I took my pills and drank water. I tried not to second guess myself, but something told me this was a flashback, not a forward movement.

Gunnar and I sat in the car, waiting for Matt to go up and knock.

No one answered. He pounded on the door.

Gunnar and I exited my SUV.

"No one is home." Matt checked the windows.

"No one been there since lunch. He packed up and flew out of here," shouted an old man from the next slip over.

Calling what the old man lived in a house was generous; it was more a of wooden shack on a dock.

"Did you know the man?" I asked.

"No, but I know evil when it squat: door. I called the owner on him. He didn': permission to be there. I was fixing to ca cops, but then, he packed up and movec The old man came closer. He wore overall a tattered undershirt and heavy rubber boc

"Was he alone?" Matt asked.

The old man shrugged. "I didn't see an' else, but that man meant to harm people. I Treater. I offered to cure him before I told to get going, but he told me get lost. I spod him good, and he left. No-good squatters."

"I'm sorry, a Treater?" I asked.

"Healer. Local folk don't trust docto: Gunnar said.

"Really?" I asked.

"Can't fix it all, but I promise to do wha can. My gift." He bowed and held up his hand

"I'm good," I lied.

"You got a black cloud on you, darlin'. I can lift it, but I can help." He put his hands on m head. "Faith. Courage. Creativity. That is you formula. You have the first two plenty."

"So, I have to be more creative?" I asked.

"Bad guys aren't always dumb." The Treate grinned and showed that he'd missed his denta checks for the last decade.

"This guy that was squatting here. Did you see him with some teenage girls?" Matt asked.

"No, but I knew I felt other beings with him. I thought maybe he was smuggling people. Illegals get in, but that guy didn't look like a coyote. Human traffickers take people out. The water is hard to police. Let that new president build a wall in my bayou. The gators will feast on him." The Treater laughed.

"Any idea where he was going?" I asked.

"Nah. He's a smart one. Keeps moving. One of those creepy vans with no windows. That should've tipped me off he was a perv with kids. If he comes back, I swear I'll whack him with my bat and then feed him to the bayou." Treater nodded.

"I'd rather you called me. You've got a name, friend?" Matt asked.

The Treater tapped my shoulder and pointed. "You've got a shadow."

I turned quick. My stalker had caught up to me. He was in his car, watching, but I felt vulnerable. He was too near, and there was no safe place to go. I'd had people out to kill me in the past but never one so calm and emotionless about it. He was like a man on a mission without feeling or thought. A robot. That was why I couldn't reason with him or argue with him. Hopefully, technology never does rise up to take over humanity, because I'd be screwed.

I started to bolt for the car, but the dock was slick, and I slipped, falling backward.

Gunnar grabbed me by the waist and hauled me against him. "Careful."

"I'm not very good at being careful in this case," I said.

"Want me to talk to him?" Matt asked.

"No, it'll just tip him off that we know he's more than a stalker. I've got a zombie out to kill me."

The Treater made some bizarre gestures and noises that resembled a man possessed with a scraggily beard and at least five hoops pierced into one ear lobe. The frail old man waved his arms and shouted words that meant nothing to me. He whooped and hollered then spun around three times.

The stalker sped off.

"Thanks!" I said.

"My land, my rules. He's got to respect that no matter what his master says." The Treater winked at me. "Get rid of that zombie. It won't help you find the girls."

"Someone just needs to tell me how," I said.

"Kill the master." The Treater shrugged.

"I'd prefer to get rid of him without killing someone," I added.

"Fine, find the master. Confront him. The curse satchel can be destroyed, and then, you can bully the master into calling off the zombie. Or you can always kill the zombie," he said.

"Slow down on killing people, okay?" Matt said and handed the Treater a card.

The Treater read the card. "Just joking about the killing people. Police understand jokes. I was simply illustrating how hard it is to remove that sort of magic without access to the source."

"Sure," Matt said.

The old man moved swiftly back to his house. Part of me was curious to know more about his work. Part of me wanted to go home and forget about my second failure.

"Should we have paid him?" I asked. "I mean, he didn't actually heal me, but he gave advice."

Gunnar shook his head. "A true Treater never accepts payment. It's their gift to help others and their blessing to do it."

"I've met plenty who take money for it," Matt said.

"Tell the locals in that area on the bayou, and they'll get run out of town. That's an affront," Gunnar said.

"How Cajun are you?" I asked Gunnar.

"Totally Cajun. I had family that grew up in the swamp. Treaters work if you believe." Gunnar sighed. "Home?"

"Where else?" I rubbed my neck.

"Call if you get anything else," Matt said.

"Your faith is astonishing," I replied.

"Your history speaks for you. One rough patch can't change that." He smiled at me.

"Thanks." I still couldn't stand up straight. My shoulder slump was beginning to feel permanent.

"Sleep will help," Gunnar said.

"If this guy keeps moving this much, I don't see how," I admitted.

"Get creative." Gunnar started up my SUV and peeled out of the bayou.

Chapter Nine

My dreams were mostly about dolls and driving around in circles. I pushed away visions of top hats and skulls. When I splashed face first in the bayou, I woke up gasping for air.

Tish hissed and scrambled for the door.

I grabbed my phone and called Matt. It wasn't me who had been tossed in the water.

He answered the phone.

"We have to go back where we were today. He dumped one of the girls in the water," I said.

"Why would he go back there?" Matt asked.

"He knows we're a step behind him. He doesn't think we'd buy him backtracking to somewhere we'd just searched. Maybe he has a friend watching it and knows it's not under surveillance. He thinks she'll be dead before we find her because we're searching elsewhere. You need a boat, divers, and a big spotlight. I'll meet you there."

"No. I'll pick you up on the way. Be out front in a few minutes," he said.

"Okay." Sometimes, I forgot Matt still lived at the big family mansion his mother reigned over. He was so not normal for a filthy rich guy; it wasn't like he had to work, but I wasn't born to this rich family dynasty crap either. Here we were serving the public good in the middle of the night.

I threw on clothes, grabbed my purse, a bottle of water, and jacket. As I tried to walk quietly down the hall, Pearl gave me away with her yipping.

"What?" Ivy asked, sticking her head out of her bedroom with a yawn.

"I found one of the girls, and we have to find her before she dies. I'll be with Matt. I'm fine," I said.

"Take Greg," she said.

"No, go back to sleep. I won't be able to rest until we've found the girls," I said.

She nodded.

I went downstairs and slipped past the zombie who'd fallen asleep in his car. I hopped in Matt's waiting car, and we were off.

With lights and sirens blaring, I wanted my seasickness pills, but we arrived in a third of the time it would have normally taken. There was a boat in the water between the Treater's shack and the abandoned houseboat with a spotlight. And a few squad cars were parked near the house we'd searched earlier.

Matt parked, and we got out.

"Anything?" he asked

"Not yet," someone shouted back.

"Got a direction?" Matt asked.

They were too far east. "Back this way. The current is pulling her this way," I said.

"Other way. I want the heat detectors over here, now!" Matt ordered.

A female officer was pointing a tool that looked like a gun at the water. She swept it methodically back and forth in a grid pattern.

We stood there and waited as the cold night air bit into our skin. I'd never been cold in New Orleans until tonight. The wind was whipping. It wasn't Chicago cold, but my light jacket wasn't cutting the midnight air. That poor girl in the water. I shivered in sympathy.

"Got her!" called the female officer running the heat seeking machine.

"Light! Divers!" Matt yelled.

An ambulance pulled up just as the divers located a form bobbing in the chilly water.

Gunnar drove in and parked after the ambulance.

"What are you doing here?" I asked.

"Ivy texted me that you were working, again. I thought I should be here." He shrugged.

"You don't have to give up your sleep," I said.

"I was here for the chase. I want to see a rescue," he said.

That I understood.

I approached as the divers handed her up on the dock to the paramedics.

"It's Kimmie. She's barely breathing," Matt said.

"She's strong," I said.

"Your tail is back," Gunnar said, jerking his head over his shoulder at a now-familiar parked car.

"He was asleep behind the wheel when I left the mansion. How did he find me here?" I asked.

Gunnar sighed. "He's got the whammy on you."

The paramedics loaded Kimmie quickly and drove off at top speed. The police were wrapping up their work, putting away their equipment.

"Let's find out." I walked up to his car and banged on the window. I was sick of wondering and worrying. Sick of feeling weak. "Get out here."

"Deanna!" Gunnar shouted.

The zombie flung open the rusty red door on his old sedan and walked out without a word.

He stalked up to me and tried to grab my arm. The contact flared some connection. He was human, and he was in there. He feared us. He feared failing. He was a ball of anxiety and inner demons. He was tormented by loud noises and PTSD.

Gunnar shoved the guy back. The two men wrestled for a bit, and the zombie seemed to be getting the upper hand. I nearly shouted for Gunnar to stop. There was nothing to be gained by those two fighting it out. The zombie's strength was impressive.

Before I could figure out what to say to stop them, Matt charged over. "Break it up. You want to go to jail?"

"Fire your pistol," I said.

"What?" Matt asked.

"Fire it. In the air, in the ground. The noise will do it," I said.

Matt fired into the soft ground three times.

The zombie screamed and staggered back. He was torn between retreating, which the human in him wanted, and completing his mission.

Gunnar took advantage of the pause and punched him in the face. The zombie reared back like he was going to punch Gunnar in return.

I grabbed the doll from my purse and twisted an arm hard.

The zombie howled and jumped back into his car. Driving with his other hand, he fled the scene.

"Are you okay?" I asked.

Gunnar nodded. "He's strong. Abnormally strong. But the doll worked. He didn't like the sound of gunfire much either."

"Yeah, weird. Look, I need to get to the hospital. Come on, De. Gunnar, you can go home. I'll get her back safe and sound. I think that zombie is done for today." Matt nudged me toward his car.

"She doesn't need to go to the hospital. She needs to sleep," Gunnar countered.

"Stop, I'm going to the hospital. I've had enough screw-ups. I want to see that the girl is okay." I patted Gunnar's shoulder. "Get some sleep. I'll need you later."

He nodded. "Watch your back," he said.

At the hospital, Kimmie's mother, Mrs. Richards, cried happy tears. That was nice to see. Kimmie was on oxygen with an IV in her arm and monitor patches all over her, including that oxygen thing clipped to a finger. The girl was moaning and restless, but who wouldn't be after being dumped in the bayou?

"We need to take off her wet things and get her warm. Please, we need a bit of privacy," a nurse said.

We stepped into the hall as they drew the privacy drape and ran into Dr. Brimlow, who was on duty in the ER. I couldn't get away from this guy.

"How is she?" I asked.

"Bad but in a weird way. She's not beaten or bruised. She's shaking." The doctor waved us behind the privacy drape and continued assessing her.

"The cold water," her mom said.

"That's part of it, but her kidnapper was also drugging the girls. Not feeding them properly. They had alcohol to drink, but he was shooting them up," I explained.

"How would you know?" Brimlow asked.

"I see things and know things. Demons and stuff," I said.

"Right." After searching Kimmie's arms, he found needle marks. "There are marks here, indicating Kimmie was injected with something. Any idea what he was giving them?"

I shook my head. "But he wasn't feeding the girls. She needs food—that's part of why she's so weak. She might have alcohol poisoning too."

"Tox screen, CBC, BA, start her on a vitamin supplement in her IV fluids and order a meal replacement shake up here from dietary. We'll see if she can drink that, but I don't want her to choke on anything while she's in this shaky stage. We'll detox her, but first, we need to know what she's got in her system. We'll get her an ICU bed, for now, but once we know the drugs, we'll be able to get her to a step-down floor with a monitored bed. She's breathing on her own, but I want her watched closely." The doc finished his orders, and the nurse took off from the private area to get them started.

Mrs. Richards nodded and held her daughter's hand. "What about the other girls, Dr. Oscar? Do you see them?"

I shrugged. "I don't see them being dumped anywhere. They're still his captives. I'm not seeing any improvement or change in how they're being treated. I don't know why he dumped Kimmie in the water. He didn't do that to the others."

Machines started beeping.

"Out, everyone. We need to put in a central line to get some meds in faster. Her BP is falling," the doc said sharply.

We all rushed out and waited.

A few minutes later, the doc walked out. "You can come back in. We just needed a more direct way to get a lot of meds in her fast. She'll need antibiotics, fluids, meds to help stabilize her blood pressure, right now. It'll be easier when we know what we're dealing with, but her heart has had some strain on it. Most drugs will do that. The infection of some of the injection sites is bad, so we'll need to have wound care look at them, as well as IV antibiotics to treat the infection."

Matt and I went back in briefly to speak to Mrs. Richards. She didn't want to leave her daughter alone, and I understood that.

"My pretty baby. That monster needs to be caught. Strung up." Mrs. Richards jaw clenched.

"I'm doing my best. I couldn't agree with you more. I'll let you spend some time with her. I'll visit tomorrow, if that's okay." I put my hand on Kimmie's foot.

"She's not going anywhere for a few days. Probably a week in cardiac IMCU." The doc nodded.

I wasn't fully listening to anyone. I hated when people talked over each other. The doctor talked about prognosis as Mrs. Richards thanked me and said to come by any time. What I felt was the unspoken pressure to find the bad guy and save the other girls.

"You okay, Deanna?" Matt asked.

I touched Kimmie's bare foot, again. It was still a bit slimy from the bayou water, but the connection to her helped me connect to her friends even better. "I know where the other girls are. They're alive." I stared at Matt. "And this girl needs a sponge bath."

"Okay, we're on it. Come on. Might see you later, Doc." Matt was already on his phone and calling for backup and SWAT as we jogged to the elevators.

I had to be right this time. These girls couldn't die.

Chapter Ten

"You're sure this time?" Matt asked.

I nodded. "The zombie's in pain. His presence and the curse cloud my abilities. Having the zombie temporarily out of commission gave me a window. It's like a section of my powers became clear, again. It won't last forever."

"When we get these girls safe, we'll figure out who cursed you. You can't keep living like this," he said.

I could blame the spider bite for my physical issues. It was the reason I was tired and achy. But my powers were being muddled by the curse. I was being stalked by a zombie programmed to kill. My life was a B horror movie.

"I probably should've gone for his leg instead of his arm," I said.

"You should've tossed him in the bayou and let the gators feast," Matt replied.

"That's not nice," I said. "You said as much to the Treater."

"He's trying to kill you. Nice isn't an option. And a man weak-minded enough to serve another and blindly obey—those are the most dangerous fools of all. Mind control and all that. He might as well be in a cult. At least, then, he wouldn't be attacking people. How do I arrest him? What has he done yet but follow you? He doesn't seem like you can reason with him," Matt ranted.

"What about that lady who ran the cult with all the snakes? She hated me." I had racked up some enemies, but many of them were dead. Whoever was behind this zombie and curse had to be alive, have a grudge against me, and be powerful.

"You think she'd wait this long to curse you? If she had the power, she'd have done it right away," Matt scoffed.

"What if she didn't have the power before? Maybe she had to build her powers and learn things. Then, she had to make herself a zombie... It could take years. Then, I was away with my brother, so it wasn't feasible from a long distance. It's possible," I said.

Matt nodded. "I'll have someone check on her in prison. See about visitors and maybe even interview her. Some people hold a grudge, but if she waited this long, I'd bet she'd wait until she got parole and do it herself. She'd want to see you suffer."

"You've got a point there," I admitted. "Turn here."

Matt screeched the tires on a sharp turn. "Come on, sunrise; more light would help."

"All the way to the end. It looks like you can't go farther, but you can," I said.

"Now, you're sounding like your old self." He slowed the car a bit as we crossed a rickety old bridge.

He stopped in front of a wall of hanging treelike limbs.

"Around there?" he asked.

"It's not solid. Go through. You can radio for backup, but he's not here," I said.

"He isn't?" Matt smacked the steering wheel.

"Sorry, but the girls are, and they need medical attention. They're all drugged and have had nothing but drugs, alcohol and maybe some crackers they scrounged for in these crap houses for days. We'll find the guy with a description from the girls and your police work." I poked his arm.

"I'm getting too old for this." He sighed and then radioed in our location for backup and ambulances.

I knew what he meant. I felt like we were constantly fighting evil and bad guys. We kept losing ground; at least, that's how it felt. Saving innocent people was a victory and important, but we never seemed to make a dent in the evil. We never beat back the bad guys and got ourselves a month off. Or even a week.

"Hold on," Matt said.

He drove through the vines and was on another earthen bridge to a shack set back from any road or dock.

"It looks like it's going to fall apart." Matt parked the car. "You're sure he's not there? No one is watching those girls?"

"Nope. The door isn't even locked. He got cocky after the last couple of days. This is so out of the way he thinks no one will ever find it. But he'll be back in an hour or so. Best to get the girls out fast," I said. During my window of clarity, touching Kimmie had given me even more insight into her kidnapper. Obviously, he'd touched Kimmie to move her so the contact gave me a better connection.

An ambulance pulled up behind us within ten minutes, and two squad cards flanked the ambulance.

"We're good to go," Matt said. "Are the girls conscious?"

I nodded. "Barely, but they're trying to find something to help. They're so weak they can't run or even stand. They're fighters, but they're afraid of men, right now. I think this guy brought a friend over. It's not sexual, but with the drugs, they'll react worse to males."

"Andrea, you first. The rest will follow. De, we'll let you know when it's clear," Matt said.

I nodded. I stood out of the way. I didn't have a weapon, anyway; I'd fallen out of habit of carrying my piece since I was back from up north. Chicago's rules about carrying were harsh comparatively, and I'd given it up. I needed to start packing more than a Voodoo doll.

Andrea pounded on the door. "NOPD! Open this door!" she shouted.

Muffled shrieks came from inside.

Andrea tried the door, and it stuck but finally opened.

I stayed in the doorway as they secured the scene. I already knew the bad guy was gone. The girls were tied up on a blanket in the corner. Huddled together, the girls were under the influence, but with it enough to realize they were being helped. Andrea knelt down and removed their gags. She reassured the girls they were safe as the other officers surrounded the house to see if they could find the kidnapper or any evidence.

"CSI?" I asked Matt.

"We'll get them in. Paramedics first," Matt said.

I moved out of the doorway. The paramedics moved in as Andrea cut away the restraints.

One of the paramedics held up a hand. "Everyone hold still."

"What? Why?" Matt asked.

The girls tried to stand, but they lacked the energy.

"Hold on." The paramedic held the girls steady. "We've got a situation. We need a snake handler," he said.

I spotted the intruder.

"Coral snake got in here." I pointed.

Corals were mean and aggressive compared to other snakes who might just want their freedom. It was snapping and hissing at everyone as the paramedics slowly eased themselves between the snake and the girls.

The girls were in the right back corner. The snake was in the middle. It had been hiding itself in trash and appeared at the shrieks of the girls.

"Is it endangered?" I asked.

Matt shook his head. "I'll get it. Everyone, please don't panic. Hold still."

"I can distract it," I offered. I picked up an empty beer bottle from the floor. Matt gave a nod, and I threw it at the left back corner. The snake struck at the sudden movement.

Matt shot three times, hitting the snake clean in the head and once in the mid-section. "Stay away from that thing."

The paramedics went back to work, and I went over to help reassure the girls. Julie wrapped herself around me and wouldn't let go.

"You guys are going to be okay. Your moms are really worried," I said.

"Kimmie?" the other girl asked weakly.

"She's alive," I replied.

"A few spider bites and bug bites, but no snakes got them. Needle marks. Let's get them in the rig, and we can start IVs en route," the male paramedic said as he used his flashlight to do a visual exam from a few feet away. "Can one of you ladies ride with them?

Matt nodded. "Andrea will ride along. Her partner can meet you at the hospital. Good work. Get the team in here. I want any evidence of this guy preserved." He pointed to the squad with two male officers. "You two find a place to stakeout. When he comes back, you grab him. Shoot him. I don't care what you do, but bring him back in alive," Matt said.

"Dead is good, too," I added.

"That's the Deanna I know." Matt smiled.

I shook my head as people scrambled in all directions and disappeared to follow Matt's directives. Our perp would try to return but once he saw the door broken down, he'd flee. The police could stake it out but the criminal wasn't dumb.

Once the girls were stabilized and we'd dealt with weepy, grateful mothers, Matt and I were able to get an update from the ever-present Dr. Brimlow.

"They're going through serious withdrawals. He was feeding these girls a lot of heroin. Kimmie is doing a bit better but still in withdrawal. We can ease the pain, but they won't be coherent for a few days. We're feeding them and giving them nutrition via IV, as well, which helps, but we have to wait and see."

"Days?" Matt kicked an empty wheelchair. "We need to know who did this to them."

Dr. Brimlow nodded. "And a police officer will be with the girls all the time until they wake up. We've modified one of our step-down monitored rooms to hold all three girls. They can be together with one officer on guard, but I can't force their recovery or clarity."

"They weren't that bad at the house." I frowned.

The doc smiled. "No, if we gave them more heroin, they'd be smiling and doing cartwheels while you questioned them. They're addicted, and they need the drug in their system to be able to function on any level. It's not their fault, but it's a very addictive drug, and they were given a lot of doses in a short time. Once it leaves their bodies, they become very ill until they get more. I can't give them more to help your case."

"Of course not," I said.

"I'm going to talk to Andrea and see what they said on the ride," Matt said.

I nodded. Dr. Brimlow walked into the ER area where the two new girls were being warmed with blankets and hooked up to various machines. I followed out of sheer determination to get as much info as I could.

"We really want to catch the guy doing this. I mean, he didn't sexually assault them or beat them up. What did he want with them? Why did he toss Kimmie?" I asked.

"She's the oldest," Julie said, slurring her words.

111

"What?" I asked.

"She's a few months older than us." Julie rocked on the hospital bed. "I want my mom."

Ms. Loupe stroked her daughter's hair. "I'm right here, honey. What did he do to Kimmie?"

"Same thing he did to all of us. Fountain of youth. She stopped giving or something. It sounds dumb, but that's what he said." Julie's head flopped back on the pillow.

"Stopped giving? Stopped giving what?" her mom prompted.

"It's like milk but it's not milk. Moo." Julie giggled.

"Do a pregnancy test," Julie's mom insisted.

"We will, but Kimmie's came back negative. There was no evidence of any sexual assault. I don't think that's it." Dr. Brimlow typed more orders in the computer.

"I'd feel it if they were pregnant. Fountain of youth," I said. "Like energy."

"Bingo!" Julie reached up and bopped my nose with her finger.

"He was sucking your energy. How?" I asked.

She shrugged. "Don't remember. Don't know. Can't remember much. Needles. Bugs. I do like tequila with lime, not the worm."

"My poor baby." Ms. Loupe petted her daughter as if to calm her.

"We'll get her medically detoxed safely. I promise. She's a victim, but it won't be pleasant." The doc checked the marks on her skin. "Nothing major from the bites. Infection from unsterilized needles."

"What do I do?" Ms. Loupe seemed more and more agitated as she got the details.

"I'm going to get you something to help you calm down. Just relax and drink some water. Your daughter is safe, and that's what really matters, now." The doc patted her shoulder and nodded for me to follow him.

"Is something wrong?" I asked as he led me into an empty room next door

"No. I'll get her a Xanax prescription. It's the shock, and watching her daughter detox will be worse. Some people are terribly panicked when a loved one is missing. Others hit a state of calm because there's not much they can do, and when the person is found, the other person falls apart because of what happened to their loved one. Still not too much they can do, so they panic and overreact. It's natural, but she'll make the nurses crazy in one night if I don't give her something. It's routine, trust me. I've sedated plenty a mother who's lost a child. Reality is a terrible thing. Now, I want to check on your neck. Save me a trip in the morning," he said.

"Right. I forgot all about it." I hopped up on a free bed. "I guess that's good."

"Yes and no." He uncovered it. "Good, you didn't scratch it and make it worse. Some people forget it's there and open the wound because it feels itchy when it heals. Be extra careful at night. Put a big bandage over it, whatever it takes to leave it alone. It's in a sensitive area. You don't want more scarring than is necessary."

"Scars don't really bother me," I said.

"Good, but reopening it can lead to infection. This one will leave you with a scar, but we want it healed." He cleaned the open wound, applied a salve of some sort, and covered it back up. "I'll check it again the day after tomorrow, but it's looking good."

"Thanks. Would it be okay if I go and see Kimmie before the other girls are moved up?" I asked.

"Sure. It'll be a few hours before we move them. They need fluids, tox screens, and some other workups for the police. Third floor, cardiac unit. Room ten."

"Cardiac?" I asked.

"The heart is what gets weakened the most by a lot of drugs dumped in your system quickly. We want them on monitored beds, so if they have any heart trouble, we catch it. Just a precaution. They're young and in good shape, but now, I have to treat them like addicts," he said.

I nodded. "Never thought of drugs being used this way."

"It's certainly not normal. Someone was dumping a lot of cash in those girls' veins." Dr. Brimlow shook his head.

That was a crazy move. I found the elevator and headed up to the third floor.

The officer on duty recognized me, so I was admitted to the room without fuss or a visitor's pass.

Kimmie was staring at the TV and giggling but her forehead was sweaty. The room actually felt chilly but she was there in nothing but a hospital gown, all the blankets were kicked off.

"Hi, Kimmie. How are you?" I sat next to her in one of those awful hospital chairs I was so familiar with.

Her head lolled toward me. "I don't know. Who are you?"

"I'm Deanna. I helped find you in the water. Can you tell me who held you captive?" I asked.

She shook her head.

"Why did he dump you in the water?" I asked.

"I wouldn't play nice." She tapped her head.

"What did he want?" I asked.

"Youth. Power. He never said exactly, but he said weird words. He touched our temples and even kissed our foreheads. I kicked him when he tried to do that. But he kept moving us. Gave me a headache. I get carsick sitting in the backseat so I was always nauseated and miserable. I don't know what he really wanted." She stared back at the TV.

"What did he look like?" I asked. "Do you know his name?"

She shook her head. "Typical middle-aged white guy."

"And he picked you guys up. He was with Uber?" I asked.

Kimmie shrugged. "A friend called a car for the four of us, but she made up with her boyfriend and decided to stay at the last minute. Lucky her."

I was making some progress, but before I could get another question out, she began slapping at the sides of her head and shrieking. A nurse dashed in and pulled her wrists into soft restraints.

"Sorry, I didn't mean to..."

The nurse nodded to the door.

I left and waited in the hall until the nurse finally exited the room after administering a medication into Kimmie's IV.

"She's doing better, but questions agitate her. The police have tried, but she changes parts of the story all the time. She's not clear, yet, and it's impossible to tell what's hallucinations and what's fact." The nurse nodded. "I know all this information is important, but we don't want her to self-harm."

"Of course not. I didn't realize she was still that fragile," I said.

"She's doing better, but sickness and anxiety are hitting her hard. The other girls coming in will only stress her out more, so you should probably let her rest," the nurse said.

"Okay, thanks." I had some information, but was it real or a drug-induced, creepy nightmare?

Chapter Eleven

A squad car dropped me off at home, and after a quick shower, I spent the day in bed. Tish and Pearl were watching my every move along with Ivy. She'd taken the day off work to make sure I got my sleep.

It's really hard to sleep when you're being watched.

Eventually, the long night of rescue with high adrenaline and no arrest caught up with me. I wanted the bad guy behind bars. It should have been enough for me that we saved the girls. They would all live. The Voodoo doll had even worked when we'd needed it. Things could be worse.

Ivy woke me up to take my pills and eat some soup and homemade sourdough bread for lunch, then promptly sent me back to bed.

It was easier to sleep after that. I crashed hard and didn't want to wake up when Ivy shook me.

"Time for dinner," she said.

"No, I need to sleep more," I yawned.

"I think you've slept too much. Matt brought that fried shrimp, French fry and garlic bread pyramid thing you like." Ivy tugged off my covers.

"I look like crap," I said.

"He doesn't care. Gunnar is here, too. He did some training at the club today, but he wanted to see how you're doing." She tossed me a hair brush. "I'll make more coffee, and we've got ice cream for dessert."

"I want cold Diet Coke," I said.

"You need brush your teeth and get downstairs. I'll have your Diet Coke and lots of cocktail sauce for the shrimp. Hurry." She shooed the animals downstairs for their dinner.

Teeth brushed, hair combed back into a ponytail and a spritz of perfume, and I headed downstairs.

Matt looked like he needed a nap. "Did you get any rest?" I asked.

He shrugged. "Big case. Lots of paperwork, and everyone wants the guy."

"I do, too, but without rest, you won't be as sharp," I said.

Gunnar and Ivy handed out the meals, and I sat, sipping my drink.

"Any leads?" I asked.

"They're still running the DNA and fibers from where we found the girls. No one has any description or name," Matt said.

I squirted ketchup on my plate then dumped some cocktail sauce next to it. I'd never get used to crawdads, but I loved fried shrimp and fries.

"Kimmie said he was a middle-aged white guy but she was still, you know...detoxing," I said.

"Not much help," Matt said. "If it's even true."

"What about the stalker? Can't we arrest him? He tried to attack De and hit Gunnar," Ivy said.

Matt shook his head. "De went after the zombie and hit his window. She provoked things. He could claim self-defense."

"He's stalking her," Greg pointed out as he turned from the stairs and joined us in the kitchen.

"I checked. He's not out front, now. I don't think he'll do that, again. I ran the plates on the car he had. Stolen. I can pick him up for that, but he'd be out in no time on bail, assuming his master will pay it." Matt sighed.

"But he won't stop. We need to draw him out. Get a name or some other information. See if we can track him back to his master," I replied.

"He had to be the one who shot at the club. He was following De; we just didn't know it, yet," Greg added.

"We need to draw him out with something public. Like a party or Mardi Gras parade," Gunnar suggested.

"We can't wait that long. Maybe a party celebrating De, that she got those girls back. Friday night. Any excuse for a party at the club." Ivy scooped up Pearl and began feeding her bits of fried shrimp. Spoiled mutt.

"No, I don't want anyone endangering themselves for me. I have the doll, but that guy could kidnap someone I care about and blackmail me into giving myself up. I'm not sure he's smart enough to do that, but if he's desperate to fulfill his orders, he might just blow up the club," I said.

"We'll have security," Matt reassured us.

"But no real grounds to arrest him. Nothing that'd hold him for more than a night. I guess we can try the party and see if he even shows up. But I don't want it to be about me. Have a pre-Mardi Gras party," I said.

Ivy rolled her eyes.

"I'll be there. Keeping an eye on De. I broke five glasses today," Gunnar said.

"Not quite Tom Cruise in Cocktail," I teased.

"In what?" Gunnar asked.

"It's an old movie. God, I'm old," I said.

"We're old. He's a baby," Greg said. "I don't like this idea of drawing out a killer."

"I'll have the doll. Worst case, I break both his legs." I smiled.

"Cool," Gunnar said.

"Steve has left you a lot of messages here. He said you're ignoring his calls," Ivy said.

"I don't have time for him. I don't need another person in danger from this crazy curse." I justified it because of the curse. I was protecting him. The truth was he didn't want to be around or he would be. If he needed an invitation to come over, he didn't get my world. People just showed up, like Gunnar and Matt.

The party was much bigger than I expected. The crush of people made me worried. The zombie could do damage to other people. He might not intend to, but did he care if he did? There were some plainclothes officers among the crowd. Gunnar was there, as well, acting as sort of a bouncer, at the moment.

Greg sat at the bar where I was hanging out. "You going to hire him for an assistant permanently?" Greg asked.

"You're too busy for the job, right now. Only some cases require both of us," I replied.

He nodded. "I know. I think it's a good idea. He's smart, safe, and not afraid to jump in."

"You approve? You won't miss me?" I teased.

"I live with you. We'll have cases together. Gunnar is what you need for muscle and driving. Steve? Well, I'm not sure he'd want the job," Greg said.

"I wouldn't offer him that job. It's too complicated," I said.

"If he's making your life more complicated, you need to cut him loose." Greg sipped a glass of soda.

He was right, but I didn't want to face it. "I'm getting too old to be alone," I admitted.

"You've got a rare calling, and not everyone will get it. But if you're going to find that right person anywhere in the world, it'll be here. Nothing is too weird in New Orleans," he said.

"True." I stared at my piece of king cake. Ivy was doing a sort of pre-Mardi Gras theme. "I still don't totally get the baby in the cake thing."

Greg laughed. "Some people move to the South, and it grows on them. You are forever Yankee."

"Damn right!" I said.

Not long after I'd enjoyed my bizarre baby-in-a-cake confection, I spotted the zombie standing stock still on the edge of the crowded dance floor. The plainclothes officers seemed to have an eye on him, as well, and Gunnar was sticking close. Matt made eye contact with me as he moved casually toward him. But there were too many people around to get in a conflict.

The zombie made his way to the bar and looked directly at me. He had a cast on his arm.

"What's your name?" I asked.

"It doesn't matter." He put his good arm on the bar.

"What's your master's name?" I asked.

"You don't need to know that either. Step outside," he commanded

"No." I assumed the zombie had orders not to kill others or not to be caught. Otherwise, he'd have lunged across the bar and strangled me by now.

"Let's take a walk outside," Greg said.

The zombie didn't move. I did, and since I had the doll in my hand, he had no choice but to follow me. I had to get that zombie out of the big group of people.

He hurried after me, as did Greg, Gunnar, and Matt. A couple of big guys I didn't recognize but assumed were cops followed behind.

"You can't stop me," the zombie said.

He lunged toward me, and as he did, I grabbed his hand. I felt a jolt of power and connection. My powers were dulled with this curse, but the more contact I had, the more I could push through and get information. I got an instant download about my zombie stalker, and it made me sad.

"Tom, you don't have to be the plaything of a master," I said.

He pulled back at the use of his name.

"You are an evil witch," he said.

He lunged at me, again, but Matt tased him.

It slowed Tom down but didn't bring him to the ground like most of us expected.

"Superhuman strength. Told you," Gunnar said.

Another cop hit him with a Taser, as well. I twisted the doll's good arm, and Tom went down on his knees.

Someone hit him with pepper spray, and the Tasers were pulled back. The cops jumped on him, trying to get him into restraints.

"You can't arrest me," he shouted.

"Stop. You have free will. Break the bond and be a good person. I don't want to have to kill you or break you more," I said.

"Witch," he screamed.

I thumped the doll's head and he went unconscious.

"He's not dead, right?" I asked one of the officers who was practically sitting on him.

"No. You knocked him out. We can put him in the drunk tank. PCP dopers act like that. The strength and all. But we can't book him," Matt said.

"I've got more on him. A feel on him. I can track him, now." I nodded. "We'll find his master. Put him in the drunk tank. I don't want him hurting anyone else tonight."

The men hauled him into the back of an unmarked SUV.

"Full name?" Matt asked.

"Tom Ginger. He's been bouncing around religions since he was a kid. He was discharged from the military. I think part of this is PTSD. Somehow, the master is relieving his trauma by controlling his mind, so to him, it's better than dealing with it." I shook my head.

"Don't feel sorry for him; he's trying to kill you," Matt reminded me.

"He doesn't want to. He just wants to keep the pain away. The mental health system in this country sucks," I said.

"He's got demons. War is hell. I've seen people bring back little demons that just mentally torture them. He'll be a drug addict or worse if he doesn't get help," Greg said.

"We can't take him home and tie him up while you try to get the demons out. That's kidnapping," I said.

Gunnar nodded.

"He wants to be around you. To kill you. He'd probably agree," Greg said.

"That's crazy. We're taking him to the drunk tank. None of the charges would stick. He'd get out in the morning, even with trying to touch you—he never made it to assault. He'll be released at seven a.m., so be on the lookout," Matt said.

I nodded.

Greg kicked a rock on the ground with malice.

"Greg, I want to help him, but we need to stay in control and out of trouble," I said.

"The world is full of demons. Little ones. Not just the mega ones that can possess people and control the dead. Minor demons who get kids hooked on drugs and tells anorexic kids they're fat. You think the voices that plague schizophrenics aren't real? They are." Greg stared up at the sky. "How? Why?"

"I've never felt a little demon. It's always big nasty ones," I said.

"Because you flick off the little ones like a gnat. It's like your spider bite. If it were a little house spider at night, you'd probably have a little itch and never look twice. It took a venomous spider to make you feel yucky, and you still kept going. You're stronger than most people. You don't see it, but you are. You can learn to see those little demons and make them run in fear of you."

"Why didn't you tell me this before?" I asked.

"You're a shrink. Mental health is a job. A science to you. And the truth is, it wasn't as bad before. It's getting worse. Exponentially worse." Greg held the cross he wore under his shirt tightly in his fingers.

"My mama says it's the end times. I figured, once we survived the Mayan thing, we were okay. But the world isn't getting better," Gunnar added.

I shrugged. "Sorry, I'm not a Bible scholar. Catholics don't really study the Book of Revelation. Jesus will come again to judge the living and the dead. That much I remember. I'm ready when he is, but I'm not running from four horsemen. If you want me to go to heaven and ask for a timetable, you do that yourself."

There was no thunder or bolt of lightning. I stood there with my friends, debating doomsday like we were some Biblical prophets.

"Only God knows the time of the end. I just want to make it better," Greg said.

"The world is getting worse. If we can help, I'm in. As your assistant or bouncer or whatever," Gunnar offered.

"Thanks. I don't even know what we're talking about. I'm under a curse, right now. I can't even overcome a stupid curse put on me by a human. You want me to play with minor demons when I can't cast off a human curse? You're nuts, Greg," I said.

I stormed into my club and had a real drink. I'd saved three girls from a bad guy. But I wasn't ready to talk about demons and end times. I couldn't keep myself free of evil. How could I free others?

Greg could take on whatever he felt, but I had to face my own demons or humans first.

Chapter Twelve

That night, Greg knocked on my bedroom door.

"I'm sorry I got annoyed. I just can't see how you think we can help all these people, right now. I'm a mess," I said.

He sat on the edge of the bed and tangled Tish's tail in in his fingers. "No, I pushed too far when I hadn't told you anything about it. I've been thinking about this stuff for a while, but I should've thought it through better. How I explained it and even brought it up—I caught you out of the blue. I'm too quiet. I keep things to myself too much."

"It's your fault? Good." I smiled.

"Don't let this thing get you down, either. Whatever locked on to you is strong and evil. Just because it's a human being behind it doesn't mean there isn't a demonic fuel somewhere. Humans can use demon energy to do things. They can lock on to someone they think deserves the punishment. It's all connected. The person probably got under your skin. You cared, so you were vulnerable. It's no wonder with your brother that you were more open and had some weak moments. All it takes a small lapse. Don't let your guard down," he said.

"I will get rid of it. But I don't know how you think we can help people with these minor demons. They aren't bad enough usually to end up inpatient at a hospital or in an institution. There isn't a place for them to go. Voluntarily or otherwise," I said.

Greg nodded. "You're absolutely right. I mean, there are rehab places for those with drugs and eating disorders. If they have the right insurance or the cash. But these little demons don't all use the same methods."

"I guess we could volunteer at rehabs. Those places are expensive. Medical insurance doesn't always cover it, and the medical coverage is in shambles, anyway, "I said.

"If only we had a rich benefactress to build whatever she wanted, staff it and offer free help. Too bad we don't know anyone like that, huh, Tish?" he asked the cat.

"Very funny. Do you understand what you're talking about? Greg, this isn't a shelter. A rehab with a religious component? We'd need a protocol," I said.

"That's your area; I'll help with the religious and counseling. Protocol is technical stuff, and you can hire a consultant to help. But those people would have a safe place to go. Take what works from traditional rehab, add the removal of those demons even if we have to put it in a metaphor for the non-believers. Get the gremlins out of your head and get in a new routine. A safe, healthy one. You could have a facility just for vets with PTSD. One for other trauma victims."

"Different protocols," I said.

"Did you blow through your Gran's fortune on your brother?" Greg asked.

"No, it's all still invested and making more. I spent a chunk on Eddie, but it's not about the money. The liability issues on this project alone—ugh." I flopped back on the pillows.

Greg nodded. "That's why I'm thinking it must be all voluntary. If they meet criteria for commitment, we hand them over to the proper facility. You have to want to be in there and sign yourself in. Go with the program."

"Drugs are one thing, but...we can't detox people." I said.

"Why not? Get some medical staff," he said.

"Malpractice and liability insurance for one. You'd need a medical staff for alcohol especially. That detox can kill people. It's not a joke or a demon. That's medical dependence," I said.

"So, we need a detox center, substance rehab, PTSD, other trauma, and eating disorder rehab so far," he said.

"It's insane. I can't imagine people are just going to sign in and trust us with their lives? Us," I said.

"You got those PhDs for nothing? Use them. Those are real credentials. I've got the religious credibility." He smiled.

"Even in New Orleans, not everyone is Catholic or Christian. You know some Christians think Catholics are freaking pagan. The Jesus followers can't all agree, and this could be a ticking bomb. It's going to be a cluster mess," I said.

"We're not forcing a religion on them. Christian core values, but all faiths are welcome. These are people who have no one to help them. Nowhere to go. If it works, they'll come." He nodded.

"We need more," I said.

"What?" he asked.

"A lot of women start using drugs or drinking when they are abused. Touched, raped, or anything in between. They numb the pain. We can't house them in a facility with men. We just can't. Crap. This is going to take a lot of planning." I opened my nightstand and pulled out a marker and a legal pad of paper.

"You want to help a lot of people, you gotta plan big. Think of all the jobs you'd be creating," he said.

"We. This is your fault. Your idea." I waved the marker at him.

Tish tried to catch the marker. Of course, it was all a game for her.

I crumpled up my first piece of paper and tossed it off the bed. Tish chased it, batting the paper around the wooden floor.

"My idea. We can name the women's one after your gran. Another one of them after your brother," he suggested.

"I hate you, right now." I started making a list.

"But you know it's a great idea. Sleep on it. Don't stress. It'll take a lot of planning. No rush." He tried to take the pad away, but I refused.

"No, I slept half the day. I need to get the basics out of my brain. I'll get to sleep by midnight. I promise," I said.

"I'll be back to check. At six, Gunnar is coming over. We're having breakfast and then going to follow that zombie. We need to track down the master."

"I'll be ready." I nodded.

"Maybe you shouldn't go," Greg suggested.

I frowned at him. "I need to confront the evil and put it in its place."

"That's the old De back." He got up and grabbed the cat. "You'll just annoy your mommy, now. I've got catnip."

I dozed, but my mind was spinning with all the ideas that Greg had thrown at me. There was no point in going forward with that crazy plan if it was so overwhelming it didn't work. Getting confirmation that it was a good idea seemed the best route. Luckily, I could go to Heaven without much more effort.

Oddly enough, as I drifted, I found myself in the waiting room of that very place. Heaven sort of had a waiting room, unless you were dead then you took another route. I'd been here plenty, but I still got uneasy about the three doors. One, I went through to Heaven, and it was safe where I saw my grandparents. The other two doors— well, one led to Hell and another to a limbo-like world where souls could stay for a while but not forever. Maybe that's where Eddie was. He had work to do, seeing as he'd sold his soul to a demon. He'd get to Heaven; I believed it. My grandparents were on the case and their parents, as well, though I'd never met that generation of my family.

I went through the safe door and ignored the others. Heaven felt like a huge futuristic city where everything was clean and shiny. There was tons of glass, and everything was bright and cheerful.

Here, people chose where they lived. Some had apartments, some little cottages, and other people needed a mansion.

I'd already sort of picked the cottage I wanted when I died. A bit bigger than the one my grandparents had with a pond in the back, but not quite as crazy big as the mansion I had, now.

I knocked on Gran's door, and it opened.

"My dear, how are you?" Gran said.

"Fine. I just needed to check on some things. Feel it out." I shrugged and looked around. "Grandpa isn't here?"

"He's with Eddie, now. We take turns, and so do his great-grandparents," she explained.

"I don't even remember them," I said.

"I'll introduce you another time. I wish I could take you to see Eddie," she said.

"I understand. I'm trying to shake this curse. I can't figure out who got the upper hand. And then, Greg wants to start something huge. I just needed a safe space." I sat in one of her overstuffed armchairs.

It felt like what I imagined sitting on a cloud would feel like.

"You're always safe here. I know the challenges are sometimes painful and frustrating, but you're allowed to go through trials for a reason. To learn or discover part of your path or make you stronger to handle the next part. I hope you get a break. It's been rough for you," she said.

"I'm tough, but I beat a demon. Now, I've got a human cursing me. My ego isn't big, but I thought I could handle things," I said.

"You thought you were above something, and it's not ego?" she asked.

"Damn. Fine. But Greg has this crazy idea to help people. I want to help them, too, but this is a huge and crazy undertaking. It's not just the money but the exposure," I said.

"You don't have to do it all at once, right? A big project can take time. If you approve. Do you want to do it?" she asked.

I sighed. "I need to know it's the right thing."

"And you're still mad about your angel?" Gran asked.

"I'm sorry; I can't figure out the angel rules. When I can ask her for something or not. When she can do something or not. So, it's like a waste, because she can't make a decision for herself. I don't need her approval, anyway. I'd rather know. You'll tell me the truth," I said.

"I will. I think you should try to get closer," Gran said.

"Oh, no. Angels are stressful enough. I'm not going anywhere near God. The big guy is out of my league. If Death's true form would kill me, I'll let you run interference, please," I said.

"Angels can't control their powers and influences. God is different."

"Still too big of a meeting for me. With a curse and zombie after me, I'm failing down there. Is this a good choice or a just a distraction that will only hurt me and Greg and everyone?" I asked.

Gran vanished.

My angel appeared.

"I don't need you, right now," I said.

"You're deliberately putting us at odds," she said.

"No, I can just make choices for myself. You can't. I feel so sorry for you. I can't imagine not having free will. Even if I screw up my life big time, I know I made those decisions, and I have to live with them. I couldn't save my brother, but I don't regret a second because I was there for him. Maybe I could've saved a dozen other people, but I needed to put my family first. I'm okay with my judgment whenever it comes. You can't understand that because you don't have a choice. Why did the big guy put angels on us if they don't really understand humans?" I asked.

"I don't know that. You'd have to ask him," Amy replied.

"Well, if you want to help tomorrow with tracking my zombie and finding the human behind it, I'll take any help I can get. I need to shake this curse, so I can find that kidnapper who took those girls. I won't let him start his creepy crimes with new girls," I said.

Gran appeared, again, and my angel left. All this popping in and out was starting to get on my nerves.

"What's wrong? You're tense," Gran said.

"My angel. I don't understand them," I said.

"You're too strong-minded to imagine blind obedience, even to God."

"That's how people end up in cults. Questions aren't disrespectful." I shrugged.

"So academic. Your plan with Greg is inspired. Don't rush it, but follow through with it. One person can only do so much. With teams of trained people, you can make a huge difference." She smiled.

I smiled, not really sure I wanted to take it all on. "Thanks. It's a lot."

"Small steps. Deal with your issue first. Make plans. Consult experts. Don't rush it, but don't use it as an excuse. Take on one task at a time and get help. Just like taking over Eddie's health situation—education, research, questions, and suggestions." She sat in a chair across from me and picked up some yarn.

"Thanks for asking. I should get back and get some sleep," I said.

She nodded. "If I could help more, I would."

"I know. Rules are rules." I hugged her and awoke back in my bedroom.

Chapter Thirteen

Over breakfast, Greg handed me a small box.

"What's this?" I asked.

"Sort of a belated birthday present. You were gone for a few years. But a friend just got back from a trip to Vatican," he said.

I opened it and found a silver crucifix on a sturdy chain. It wasn't a dainty little cross, but it wasn't too huge. "The Vatican?"

"Yep, he had an audience with the new Pope. It was personally blessed," Greg said.

"Pulling out the big guns," Ivy said.

"Can't hurt," Greg said as he came around the table to put it on me.

"Thanks for the thought. It's nice." I appreciated it, but I didn't want my friends to feel like they needed to protect me.

"We better get going to follow that zombie," Gunnar said.

"I'll trust you guys to handle it. I need to be at the club," Ivy said.

Gunnar drove, and Greg tagged along. We waited across the street from the police station, not wanting to tip him off.

The zombie finally emerged from the station, sometime later, and Gunnar followed him, creeping along at an unnoticeable distance. He drove for what seemed like miles before turning down a street in a questionable neighborhood. He parked, then went into the back of a small old home with a sign out front that read "Voodoo Practitioner: True Believers Only."

"Back or front?" Greg asked.

"You go front; we'll go back," I said.

Gunnar circled around and parked half a block away. Greg took off for the front as Gunnar knocked sharply on the back door.

A guy so pale he looked like he belonged to the Malfoy family answered. "Can I help you?"

"We just wanted to make sure that your zombie got home okay. We need to chat about you lifting this curse," I said.

"Dr. Oscar, I presume," he said.

"You cursed me, and you didn't know me?" I moved inside past him without invitation.

Gunnar stayed close by.

"Please sit down. I assume he is with you?" The blond man pointed to Greg, who had nudged his way into the back from around the front counter.

"He is. Call off the zombie. Remove the curse. I don't know what I did to you, but I never meant to hurt you, unless you're really evil." I shrugged.

"Oh, you did nothing to me. I was hired to do this job. I can't lift the curse, because I don't have the items any longer. But since this zombie has failed..." He snapped his fingers.

The zombie walked out.

"You job is over. You failed. Return to your routine until I need you, again." The man clapped his hands.

The zombie shook his head, and the mental fog seemed to lift from him. He ran for the back door and bolted outside.

"That's one thing down," Gunnar said.

"If you believe it," I replied.

"You have no faith in me?" the zombie master asked.

"You haven't even told me your name," I said.

"Forgive me. Lester Norcowski."

"Why would you remove the zombie just because we requested?" Gunnar asked.

"He was ineffective. You had a Voodoo doll, clearly. Breaking his arm takes amazing strength. So, he couldn't succeed. He could only distract you. The curse is still intact. I can't help you there. You must find the one who put the spell into motion and end it there," he said.

"That's your business? Programming zombies to kill and conjuring curses for others?" Greg asked.

"Everyone has to make a living." He shrugged.

"Who cursed me?" I asked.

"I can't tell you that. Clients pay for discretion. Or else I could just have had you pay me more to not put one on you, at all. Or charge you a lot to reveal my client. I don't do that."

"So, you are loyal and have ethics?" Gunnar laughed.

"Honor among thieves. She goes around helping people for free. I used to do it, too, but that business has dried up," he said with a sigh.

I looked around. "There is more going on here than Voodoo," I said.

Lester shrugged. "Santeria is popular, as well. I see you're Catholic. It's a nice blended religion."

"Not interested. I was thinking more like Hoodoo. I feel a pull of power like a vortex around here," I replied.

"Hoodoo isn't much of a religion. It's a power gain. I don't deny I've dabbled in it plenty. It's a rush," he said.

"Is this person trying to kill me?" I asked, hoping to get the conversation back on topic.

"The zombie already tried. You've upset someone. But you're smart enough to put them in their place. I can't help you with details. But there was no fear or remorse in your enemy. They felt wronged and justified to get you out of their way. Beware false friends and easy answers."

Gunnar's expression said he wanted to punch the guy in the face.

"Old or new enemy?" I asked.

"New. This person doesn't know the power of the one they are attacking. I'm sure you'll show them. But your powers have grown. I have no wish to cross you," he said.

"I'm not a Hoodoo practitioner," I said.

"No, you don't covet power for power's sake. You have untapped power because you honor only the good. Seek clarity and protection, and you'll find your offender. I'm not sure what you'll do with them when you catch them. It's a tricky crime to prosecute." Lester smiled and opened the back door. "Now, if you please. I don't like nonbelievers in my house for long. Ruins the vibe."

I stood and nodded. Greg went first. I made it to the doorway before turning back. "Gunnar, go ahead."

Gunnar punched Lester once in the face, and he went down like a twig. "No more curses or messing with us," he said.

Lester was out cold.

"Thanks," I said to Gunnar.

"He deserved worse." Gunnar escorted me out carefully.

Back at home, I kept the Voodoo doll, just in case.

"The doc should be here any minute. Then, we can do whatever. What do you want to do today?" Gunnar asked.

"Let me think about it." I grabbed a yogurt from the fridge and poked at the goo with a spoon until the doorbell rang.

"You don't look too happy to see me," Brimlow said.

"It's not you, Doctor. I just don't seem to have the luck lately. Things are complicated," I said.

"Well, this spider bite is looking better. This should be the last day I have to trim anything, and you can just keep it covered with ointment during the day. Let it get air at night." He went to work on my neck.

"Do you ever wish you didn't have to deal with insurance and all the red tape?" I asked.

"Well, the hospital and my staff usually does that. But, yes. I donate my time at shelters and such, but you have to pay the bills, even doctors. Medical school is a fortune, and malpractice insurance isn't cheap," he said.

"Yeah, but everyone gets sick. Everyone needs helps, sometimes." I sighed.

"True, but I'm not worried about you paying your bill," he teased.

"No, that's not my problem. But everyone has problems. Everyone gets challenged," I said.

"That's how we learn. It can be frustrating, but it makes you better." He nodded. "All done. Stay away from those spiders."

"Thanks, Doc." I walked him out.

When I came back to the kitchen, Gunnar was eating my yogurt.

"I thought it was up for grabs," he said.

"It is. When you're done, I know where I need to go," I said.

Gunnar parked in the lot, and I got out. He followed.

"You're sure it's open?" he asked.

"It's a church." I threw him a look that said he'd grown three heads.

"What church is always open?" he asked.

"Catholic ones," I answered as I opened the big, ornately carved door.

The smell of candles and incense were like a time machine back to grade school.

"What are we doing here?" he asked softly as I dunked my fingers in the holy water.

"I need to block that curse. I need protection. You can look around—give me a few minutes." I slid into a pew and crossed myself.

"Okay." He started wandering around the church, looking at the statues and stained glass.

"Whatever curse or hex anyone put on me is no good here. So, who did it? Why?" I asked softly.

I closed my eyes and let the visions come. My zombie, his wounds from the army. His tortured mind. I felt sorry for him; the fear was completely gone. Then, I saw the creepy Lester. He was in it for the money and the power, but he'd kept the secret of his employer carefully blocked. I focused on his mind and got the impression of a young and insistent female.

She didn't just want me cursed or dead. She wanted the power of Hoodoo. The girl was more than a client; she was his apprentice. It was forbidden, somehow, but they managed to find the time to share lessons. She loved the zombie angle. Young and impressionable. I couldn't see her or put my finger on why anyone like that would want me dead.

Then, another vision took over. The bad guy was still on the loose. The kidnapper had cut his losses last time because we were so close. The police were still looking, but the girls had been so out of it, none had a good look at him. The man was now free to stalk other young girls. His face was always in the shadows. He kept it hidden. He was using their energy. What for?

I lost the connection. The guy had gifts. He knew when I connected to him. No wonder he always fled before a breakthrough.

I sat back and took a deep breath.

Looking around for Gunnar, I found him studying the stations on the perimeter of the church.

When my energy returned, I joined him. "Crown of Thorns. Fun."

"What is this?" he asked.

"Stations of the Cross. Jesus' torture and death all the way around. The fun of every Friday in Lent at Catholic school. You think Mass is a stand, sit and kneel fest? This is worse." We followed the path around the church.

"Jesus falls," he read. "This is rough."

The little plaques were detailed. "Yep. Want to keep going? Or we can leave," I offered.

He nodded. "This is depressing."

I muffled a laugh. "The ending is happy. I promise."

Gunnar smirked. "Where to?"

Chapter Fourteen

Gunnar made sure that I had a decent lunch and sent me to bed for a nap. It was overkill to me since I'd been released by the doctor. Still, I did sleep a little before something began nagging at me. The curse or something else?

No, my own conscience was getting at me. The girls were safe, but their kidnapper was still on the loose. I found my phone under a sleeping kitty and called Matt.

"Hey, how's the curse?" he asked.

I laughed. "Still around. The zombie has been called off because I have the Voodoo doll. Other than that, the master denied everything.

We can't prove anything. I have his address if you want to keep an eye on him, but right now, I'm more worried about that kidnapper out there. He's not going to give up."

"I know. The girls are better, but they were kept high and drunk. He was careful. No prints. No DNA. The guy didn't rape them or hurt them. The girls just report being exhausted all the time. He would touch their heads."

"He's doing some sort of ritual. Black magic or Hoodoo. I don't know what, but I think he is using them for energy or power. The girls might take a while to get their energy back. I don't know what was truly done to them, so they might be weakened going forward," I said.

"We need to get the bastard," he said.

"He didn't own any of those shacks?" I asked.

"No. Half were abandoned. The mothers want justice. I don't have a lead. Even if you got me on the right track, we'd have to find the evidence to charge him. I've got nothing to tie anyone to it. Maybe if he still has the van, but the girls just remember the SUV he picked them up in, thinking it was an Uber." He sighed.

"So, he wasn't making friends with them or grooming them to trust him before? No one from their school?" I asked.

"No, no one suspicious in their lives. We've been interviewing them gently but routinely. I don't want to wait for the guy to strike, again, but right now, we don't have enough to prosecute, even if I had his name," Matt said.

"Sucks," I said.

"It does. If you come up with anything, let me know," he said.

"Okay, thanks. Bye." I ended the call in frustration.

Unable to sleep, I called Gunnar.

"What's up?" he asked.

"I want to go drive around. See if I can feel the kidnapper," I said.

"I don't think that's the best idea," he said.

"Fine, I'll drive myself," I replied.

"No, now, hang on. I think you've worked yourself too hard. Your brain is all twisted up," he said as he walked into my bedroom.

What? "I thought you went home." I swiped to end the call and put the phone down.

"No, I need to keep an eye on you. You've been through a lot between spiders and finding the girls. The curse and a zombie. You don't need to go driving off randomly, hoping to find the guy. You're muddled as it is, and wasting your energy only helps them," he said.

I knew he was right. "I can't sit in bed, anymore. The curse isn't a sickness. The spider thing? Fine. I might be somewhat allergic to some spider bites. But I'm fine, now. The doc cleared me. I need to get back to normal," I insisted.

"Okay. I've only known you a short time. Feels like forever, but what do you normally do?" he asked.

"Work."

"That's part of the problem. You need to relax. Have a little fun. Don't let that curse ruin your life or rule it. Just because one gift is a bit fuzzy, it's not your whole life," he said.

"Yes, it is. I have some other gifts, but they won't find the kidnapper," I said.

"I'm more interested in who cursed you, right now. Solve that, clear the curse, and bingo. You'll have that kidnapper in no time."

I sat back and smiled. "You're right. How did you get so good at this?"

"Cop training is pretty good at the police academy. Work the lead that has traction instead of spinning your wheels on taxpayer time."

"That sounds like something Matt would say," I agreed.

"I think if you eat a good meal, go to the club and have a few drinks, dance a bit and unclench your brain—you might figure out who cursed you. Focus on fun and let your subconscious work it out," he said.

"Maybe you just want to go dancing?" I teased.

He shrugged. "I can go home and let you dance. Ivy said you have a boyfriend named Steve. Go out with him."

"He's not really my boyfriend. We went out for a while, but I got back into my work. Since then, it's only been a few dates. He just doesn't fit in." I toyed with the kitty's tail, and she whacked my finger with her paw.

"Give him a shot. Do I fit in, yet?" he asked.

"Oddly, yes. Fine. Pizza and then the club," I said. "You're driving so I can have a couple drinks."

"Deal." He nodded.

New Orleans pizza could never compare to Chicago pizza, but they tried, and it was comfort food. Gunnar had forced me into a long black dress which got me a lot of compliments at the club.

I sat at the bar and sipped a Grasshopper. It was vintage drink night or something.

"Maybe it's some weird religious person who thinks your powers are demonic?" Ivy asked.

"They wouldn't use a Hoodoo or Voodoo practitioner to curse me. Would they/" I asked.

"No, I guess not. Or would they fight fire with fire? I don't know. Maybe it's a cop? You solve their cases before they do, sometimes. Maybe you showed someone up, and they held a grudge?" Greg suggested.

"Is it worth their careers? Matt trusts me, and they know that. No, it has to be someone with a big enough reason. I need another drink." I finished off the one I had.

"You need to dance," Gunnar said.

He pulled me off the barstool and into the group on the dance floor.

I indulged him. He was a great dancer, hot, and I was the envy of everyone in the room. At least he kept his clothes on for this dance.

The next morning, I woke with a slight headache, a serious thirst, and a name.

I downed half a bottle of water while I texted Gunnar.

While the kitty licked at the bottle, I heard footsteps.

Gunnar poked his head in my room. "Ready when you are. Breakfast is ready, too."

"You spent the night? Where?" I asked.

"One of the guest rooms. You've got like ten in this place," he said with a smirk.

"Not quite that many. I'll shower and change. You and Ivy aren't..." It wasn't my business, but I couldn't help but ask.

"No, she's great. I like guys who are guys all the time. I know my generation is all about fluid this and pansexual that, but I'm just a boring guy who likes guys." Gunnar shrugged. "See you downstairs."

Half an hour later, we were on the road. I didn't want to go alone, and Greg was still sleeping. He'd gotten into some drinking game watching a show and had more than he should've.

I never thought I'd be back at Chet's home. We'd cleared his bar of some nasty demons with a group called the Ghost Tamers. It'd been Ivy's doing, mixing me up with a reality TV show of ghost hunters. There were tons already on TV, but Ivy thought it'd help my return to New Orleans. I'd met Steve through them, but the truth was, I wasn't meant to be on someone else's team. I'd done the job because that bar had been so horribly haunted with ghosts using and controlling other ghosts along with a demon that mentally compromised and tortured many members of the staff. It had taken a lot of work to clean that building, and Chet's teenage daughter Tanya hadn't wanted it fixed. She fed on the activity or it fed on her. Talk about a codependent relationship.

Chet hadn't minded the paranormal activity; some people are barely affected by what will make someone else very weak and ill. Chet blocked it out. His daughter fed on it. Luckily, Chet wanted his employees to stick around and his customers to be safe, so he'd let every floor in the entire building be cleared of anything supernatural. Tanya hadn't been happy about it, at all.

"Deanna, how nice to see you. Is everything okay?" Chet asked.

"No, I'm sorry. It's not okay. This is my assistant, Gunnar. I need to see Tanya," I said.

"Of course, come into the kitchen. Have some coffee," he said.

We followed him into the kitchen. "Tanya, get down here," he shouted.

She took her sweet time, but she finally turned the corner and stared at me like I was a ghost.

"Don't run. I'll stop you," I said with a smile.

"Run? Why would she run?" Chet asked. "She's getting straight As and spending more time with friends, now. Isn't that right?"

"Yeah, I'm all good. What are you doing here?" Tanya asked.

"I had someone put a curse on me. A pretty nasty one that involved clouding my abilities. There was even a zombie trying to kill me," I replied.

"How awful. I hope you got rid of it. You handled demons so well—a little curse isn't hard," Chet said.

"Well, you see, curses are tricky, and I'm not an expert on the occult. Good and evil is one thing, but humans aren't black and white. This was done by a human who wanted me dead. I found the zombie master, but he can't break the curse because he gave the person who hired him all the objects she'd need to maintain the curse. I need that satchel to neutralize it." I stared at Tanya pointedly.

"Good luck finding it. What does it have to do with us?" Chet asked.

"I'd like to search Tanya's room. She didn't like giving up her ghosts and games. She might be just hiding it all from you," I said.

"No way. No way you get in my room," she denied in a panicked tone.

Chet stood. "I do. Let's go look," he replied.

He led the way to her room, and I followed, feeling the swirl of paranormal power grow stronger. Tanya hadn't been a victim of what was in the bar. She had gifts, and she was using them for the wrong reasons. The demon activity in the bar had clouded Tanya's skills or Tanya hid them well. Either way, the truth was about to come out.

"You think I'd be that dumb to curse her? She knows me. Of course she'd blame me. I'm an easy target," Tanya ranted behind me.

Chet went for under the bed. I ignored the teen and went for the closet.

"Get out of there!" she yelled.

Gunnar stood between her and me, but he was smart; he never put a finger on the teen.

"Tanya, you're interested in unusual things. I like that, but you need to respect powers, and some things aren't to be messed with." Her father dumped a Ouija board and tarot cards on the bed.

"People make a living doing that in the French Quarter," she argued.

I opened a couple of shoeboxes up on a shelf. "Crystals. Black candles. Voodoo doll, not of me, thankfully. Satchel."

I tossed the other stuff down but held on to the satchel.

"You had a Voodoo doll. Hypocrite," she said.

"How do you know she had one?" Gunnar asked.

Tanya's face burned red.

Chet moved to stand over his daughter. "How did you know? How did you get one? Those aren't games."

"She's studying Hoodoo. I've met her master, Lester," I said.

"He's not my master. He has the zombie. I don't obey. I'm just learning things." She shrugged.

152

"When? When do you learn from this man?" Chet asked.

"You think I'm with my friends. Lester is my friend. He's so strong and smart. I'm growing my powers. I did the curse. It's no big deal." She shrugged.

"Lying to me is. You're seeing grown men. Who knows what could've happened to you? You could hurt people without thinking it through. This Lester might be setting you up for some of his bad deeds."

"I'm not stupid. Just because I'm not an adult, yet, everyone thinks I'm a fool," she shot back.

"I don't think you're a fool. I think you want power no matter how you get it. That's not the right way. You'll carry the consequences of dark magic and hurting people. That never goes away," I said.

"Lester said the goody-goody people would say that. I'll turn evil. It's not like I sacrificed a house pet or anything. It worked." She grinned.

I opened the satchel a bit and smelled death. I saw little bones. "Bird bones?"

"She's sick," Gunnar said.

"No, I did it right." She tried to grab the satchel from me.

Chat grabbed her arm. "Where did you get the money for this? How did you pay for these lessons? Does he do it for free?"

"I handle my business." Tanya folded her arms stubbornly across her chest.

Gunnar kept going through the closet. "Found some books."

"Get out of my room!" Tanya shrieked.

Chet grabbed her keys, phone, laptop, and purse. "You bring out everything that is related to this stuff. Put it on your bed, so I can go over it. You won't see Lester, again, until I meet him. Don't try to get out the window. I'll be watching."

Tanya pursed her lips and didn't respond.

Chet escorted us back downstairs.

"I'm sorry. I can't believe she cursed you." Chet leaned on the kitchen counter. "What else is she doing?"

"I don't know. She's put my powers on the fritz, and that's part of the problem. She could have cursed girls at school or who knows what. There's nothing illegal that I can see to have her arrested for, but she needs to be brought under control," I said.

"She's a little girl. That guy is the problem," Chet said.

A blind parent who thought their child was perfect or the victim when they misstepped couldn't be reasoned with.

"She tried to have me killed. That zombie was out to attack me," I said.

"I'm sure it was just a prank. An exaggeration. There's no proof," he said.

"You need to get your daughter under control. She could hurt someone, including you if she doesn't like your rules. The more power she develops that goes unchecked, she could do real damage to you, your business, or innocent people out there. If she does that, I will find a way to have her arrested and kept in juvie," I threatened.

"I think you have what you came for. Please go," Chet said.

Gunnar tugged on my arm. "Time to go, De."

Chapter Fifteen

Gunnar drove straight to the Voodoo shop we'd visited a few days back. Tamara actually looked relieved when I walked in.

"Is this it?" I asked, putting the satchel on the counter.

"That's it. Who is your hater?" I saw strands of my hair as she spread the contents on the counter.

"A teenager. I cleared her father's bar a while back of ghosts and a demon. She liked the ghosts and power fix. She's looking for it elsewhere," I said.

"And the parents think the girl is innocent or a victim. I see this too much. I swear—the online bullying and some kids killing themselves over it has to have curses and dark magic fueling it," she said.

"I'm sure you're right. I don't know what to do. There's no real crime. She's underage, too. She hates me, so I can't do much. It's up to her father, right now. But I need to protect myself," I said.

She nodded. "Do you have the Voodoo doll?"

I handed that over.

"I can't share the rituals. But while I neutralize the curse, you should pray for protection from that girl," Tamara said.

I held onto the crucifix around my neck and focused on the protection. My guardian angel showed up. So nice of her to actually appear for a change.

"You're not done with that girl," Amy declared.

"I need protection from her. She's bad," I said.

The angel nodded and touched my head. I felt a glow. All the darkness and cloudiness was gone.

When I opened my eyes, the angel was gone. Gunnar stood there quietly. "Weird."

"Yeah. My guardian angel finally turned up and helped," I said.

"You have a difficult angel?" he asked.

"I think so. But I'm probably as difficult. She drew the short straw." I laughed. "Did you see anything?"

He shook his head. "You were talking to someone else and sort of froze. But you see ghosts and stuff. I have to get used to that if I want to be your assistant," he said.

"You really want this job permanently?" I asked.

"I sucked at tending bar. I don't mind stripping, but you're helping people. You're doing real stuff. I can dance, if I need more money, on nights you don't need me, but I'd rather be around. Keep you out of trouble," he said.

"Okay, you're hired. I'll talk to Ivy about what she was paying you. If you made good money stripping, why did you drive a beat-up car?" I asked.

He shrugged. "Sometimes, I do jobs in areas that aren't the best. I don't want to get a nice car stolen. It's pretty reliable, just older."

"I'll get you an SUV. Company car." I shrugged.

"No, you don't have to," he said.

"I do. I need you to be there when I need you. No car trouble excuses. It could be two in the morning and certainly any weekend," I said.

"And it could be a ghost, demon, possession or murder. That's the cool part. Not knowing. Stripping? I know pretty much what it'll be. As soon as I get to the place, I know what sort of group I have. I liked the unpredictability of being a cop. You'll pay better." He grinned.

"True." I nodded.

Tamara walked out from behind the curtain. "It's done. This is for you."

She handed me another Voodoo doll.

"Tanya?" I asked.

"Yes. If she is using dark magics to torment you, you must have a way to keep her in line. Use it with caution, but I felt her determination to have great power and use it. There must be a way to check her. Until then, you have this," she said.

"Thanks, Tamara. You're sure I can't pay you?" I asked.

She shook her head. "You found those girls."

"I didn't get the kidnapper, yet." I sighed.

"You will," Tamara nodded. She returned to the back of her shop.

"Thanks, again," I shouted.

I felt a million times better, but right now, that had me convinced something else was going to hit me. The odd thing was Steve left a message on my cell while I was in the Voodoo shop. He wanted to have dinner.

I met him at an Italian place. We had a back booth, and that was probably best.

"I haven't heard from you in a while," he said.

"I've been busy with a curse and Voodoo stuff," I said.

"We did another case. The Ghost Tamers would like to follow you, again," he replied.

The waitress came up, and I went ahead and ordered. I wasn't going to drag this night out. I wanted to enjoy the release, not explain myself.

When the waitress left, I started in with my side of things. "I'm not interested in being filmed, again. I have my own cases. I'm sorry I've been quiet, but you have your group, and I have mine. We don't really fit in with each other's friends." I shrugged.

"And that means we can't date? Talk?" he asked.

"I don't think dating is working. If it's this much work to be on the same page, we're not working. I'm not going to force a relationship. My work is the most important thing to me next to my family. I neglected my work for my family for a long time. Now, I have to do what's right for me." I sipped my water.

158

"I get that. But you're running around town with a stripper. You think I wouldn't find that out?" he asked.

"I don't care what you find out. He's my new assistant. Gunnar also used to be a police officer. He's got the skills. And he fits in with my group."

"Yeah, I believe that," he said.

"What does that mean?" I shot back.

The waitress brought out salads and garlic bread.

When she left again Steve jumped right in. "You have a drag queen, a former priest, a psychic, and now, a stripper as your entourage. It's crazy."

"Then, why did you ever ask me out? This is me. Those are my friends. You think I'm just hanging out with them until I find more normal friends? I will never be normal. My powers are growing. My life will only get more complicated. And I'm not hurting for cash where I need to do a TV show." I stabbed my salad, hating how that last sentence sounded.

"But you could fund a show. A few of them. You could invest in groups. You could be huge in the paranormal studies world," he said.

"That's why you were dating me?" I asked.

"No," he said.

"And we haven't talked in a while, but you called and wanted to see me to give me grief. Why not let this just fizzle out and not call?" I asked.

He focused on his food. "I have bad timing."

"No, you're lying," I said.

"Stay out of my head. That's rude," he shot back.

"If you can't handle that, you definitely can't handle me. I bet it was the Ghost Tamers.

They need a boost or want something. They're pushing you to keep the contact. Well, forget it. I'm not doing anything else with other groups. If I'm not in charge of it, I'm not playing along," I said.

"They said you really were Garden District. Rich and powerful." He put his napkin on the table.

"I inherited it all, but I'm not going to hand it over to others. I won't be bullied into things because I have the means. You can't guilt me or play me." I folded my arms.

"Got it. We're done," he said.

"No kidding," I said as he left.

The waitress came up. "Everything okay?" she asked.

"Fine. He's history. I'll finish my salad and take the entrees to go, if that's okay," I said.

"Sure. How about dessert on the house?" she said.

"That's sweet, but I'm really kind of relieved that he split. Do you have cheesecake?" I asked.

"We have a strawberry cheesecake. I'll cut you a big piece." She cleared away Steve's salad.

"No, pack up a whole cheesecake. I'll pay for it. I'm taking the dinners home and sharing them with my friends. Add a big order of garlic bread and a double order of traditional spaghetti, please," I said.

"Sounds like a plan," she said.

I texted Ivy and Greg to be ready for pasta. Not many men could handle a psychic girlfriend who rushed off after cases of murder, kidnapping or hauntings. Add in being rich and knowing my own mind, and the right man might not be out there for me. I stabbed the croutons. Was this what it felt like to be a nun? I couldn't cut the habit. Poverty and obedience weren't my strong areas. But right now, no boyfriend felt better. I looked up at the ceiling. "If you send the right one, fine. I'm not looking, anymore."

The waitress approached with two bulging bags. "Did you say something?"

"Talking to myself. Better conversation than my ex." I handed her a credit card.

"I bet. I'll be right back." She dashed off.

I gave her a big tip and carried home a lot of carbs. As a bunch of single people trying to help others and stop evil, we'd burn off the calories and deserved to be well-fueled.

Chapter Sixteen

Full of pasta, wine had Ivy opened, and cheesecake which was a dumped girl's right, I slept like the dead. The good dead. No curse, no drama, and no stress.

When my phone rang before eight a.m., I knew that bliss was gone.

"Hi, Matt," I said without opening my eyes. Being psychic had its advantages.

"Two girls were reported missing this morning. Mothers said they talked to them last night. They went to a party with friends. They were going to Uber home and never turned up. They checked with all their friends, and no one has seen them," Matt said.

"Yeah, that's our guy. He won't backtrack to the old places. He'll find a new place. Give me the names," I said.

"Terry and Soli Carson. They're cousins."

I focused on the cousins and found them in a van, holding hands and trying to stay awake. "He's drugged them and got them in the back of the van. Same crappy van."

"Give me a description or plates—if you can," Matt said.

I pulled out from the inside of the van to look at the back. "It's white with rust around the back doors. Cargo. The plate is a New Orleans Saints plate—all fives."

"Got it. Perry Braden. Forty-five. Priors for theft and kidnapping, but they were years ago. He's not on parole. Any idea where he is?" Matt asked.

"He's heading for something called Lake Lery. You guys have too many damn lakes," I complained.

"That's good. I'll meet you there," he said and ended the call.

I texted Gunnar to get over here. We had work to do.

Half an hour later, I stood by a lake. It wasn't a Great Lake, by any means, but it was a good-sized lake. Some shacks dotted the edges. I wasn't sure if anyone lived in them. Maybe they were for fishing or something.

"Got a feel?" Matt asked.

I surveyed the options. "You can't find the van?" I teased.

"My guys are circling."

"That one." I pointed to a small shack with lots of tree cover.

Matt's radio crackled with the voice of one of his men. "We've got a white van in a lot of tree brush. Across from your position."

"Good. We're heading over. You two hang back," he replied.

"Perry sees you. He's going to bail," I said.

Matt and the police rushed to their vehicles and sped to the house. An ambulance followed at a safe distance.

"Where do we go?" Gunnar asked.

"Wait here. The cops will get the girls—the guy is going to bail on a motorcycle. He knows these swamps. We can't follow him in a car," I said.

Not getting in the way, I watched the cops bust in as Perry bailed out the side and hopped on a motorcycle parked out back. He sped off south. Gunnar and I pointed in the right direction when the cops came out in pursuit. Once Perry was gone, the danger was gone. I walked up to the house.

"Follow him," Matt ordered a squad.

"He's going through the swamps," I warned.

The girls were shaking and confused, just as I expected. They were in better shape than the first batch of girls we'd rescued.

"He was the driver. We were just taking an Uber home," cried one of the girls.

"He didn't do a very good job, did he?" I asked.

"My mom is going to be pissed," said the other.

"No one is mad at you. This guy did the same thing to three other girls. Do you have your phones? Do you have an Uber text?" I asked.

One of the girls pointed to a box on a shelf. "He took all our stuff and put it up there."

A cop with gloves on grabbed the phones and began scrolling through them. "No Uber texts."

"Our friend ordered the ride for us. Can I have some water?" she asked.

The paramedics moved in with water and checked the girls over.

"Is your friend here, too? Did she get away?" Matt asked.

The other girl shook her head. "Soli wanted to go. I was bored, too. Tanya had a fight with her boyfriend and ordered the car. Then, I guess they made up before the car got there. She wanted to stay with her man. We just took the car. We thought it was a safe service. Our mom said it was okay to use it to come home. We were going to pay," Terry sobbed.

"You were set up," I said.

Gunnar looked at me. "Tanya."

"Is this guy really an Uber driver? Is he using that as a cover? Or did Tanya tell him to pose as one?" I asked.

Matt nodded. "We'll find out after we locate him. Tanya? That was the name of the girl the other three were hanging with. She ordered both Ubers." Understanding crossed his features. "Oh, hell."

"She's also the one who cursed me. Set that zombie on me," I said.

"Get these girls to the hospital. We'll get photo of this girl Tanya and a warrant."

"I have a picture of her." I pulled it up on my phone. "Her dad owns a haunted bar. She liked the haunting and got hung up on the power of evil and ghosts. Is this your friend?" I asked the girls.

"Yeah. She's just another girl from school. We weren't going to turn down a ride. It's not like it was a guy trying to get us in the backseat." Soli shrugged.

"You girls didn't do anything wrong, but I'd order your own Ubers from now on. Did he touch you? Hurt you?" Matt asked.

The girls shook their heads.

"Just made us drink liquor and shot us with drugs. I don't remember much of the ride home," Soli said.

"We'll take you to the hospital to check you out. Get you hydrated and fed. Get your moms to bring you clean clothes," said a paramedic.

"She'll be so mad," Soli said.

"No, I'll speak to them. No one will be mad as long as we get this guy." Matt looked at me.

"We'll need a boat," I said. I stifled a smile, but it felt so good to be clear. It had been a long time.

And now, we had something on Tanya. Somehow, this was all connected. She was using these girls to practice her spells and curses? I wasn't sure, yet, but the police would bring her in and charge her. She was at least an accessory to kidnapping of minors.

Not much later, we were on a boat tracking the pier to a boat house in the swamplands. Hanging trees, hissing snakes, the whole scary movie setup. I didn't like it, at all. But this guy was a lifer. He belonged on Swamp People. He knew this place and counted on the critters and water to keep people away.

"Two more slips," I said and pulled my hair back in a ponytail.

"Surround the shack," Matt ordered.

The SWAT team went off the boat first. They were a wall of shields and body armor. I projected myself into the room. None of them could see me. The bad guy had guns, knives, and charms. He was ready for anything, except he was alone. The SWAT team breached the door, and Perry started shooting them, but the bullets bounced off the shields, and the team surrounded the guy before he could get away. They wrestled him to the ground. Perry got in a few good punches, but they had him tied up fast.

The team secured all the weapons and searched the suspect.

"Clear," the leader said. "Pick him up and secure him in a vehicle."

I returned to my body as they brought him out. Gunnar was looking at me funny, but I'd explain my ability to go out of body later. That was an awkward chat.

We watched at a safe distance. The guy struggled hard, even hogtied. As they carried him out, he lunged his head toward me as if to bite.

I jumped away as Gunnar caught me and braced us on a tree.

"You're good, but you're not perfect. We got to you. Got in you. My master could hurt you," the guy snarled from his upside-down position.

"Lester? Not really that scary," I said.

"Hang on," Gunnar said.

"What?" I asked.

"Something crawling under your shirt. Hold still," he said.

"Under?" I wiggled my shoulders, no matter how hard I tried to stop. "The shirt is white—you should be able to see it."

"It's black and a spider," Gunnar said.

"Kill it," I shrieked. "Ouch—"

He smacked me hard and swore. "Got it."

168

"Too late." I said.

Matt gave us an evidence bag and plastic glove. "You got the spider whammy."

"Black widow." Gunnar used a glove to retrieve the body and put it in the bag. "Hospital? We need to check on the other girls, anyway."

"I hate spiders." I scratched the area unconsciously.

"Don't touch it," Gunnar said.

"See you at the hospital. We've got to speak with the other girls. Verify the connection. Then, I'll work on getting the warrant and then arrest Tanya. Maybe this Lester guy, too," Matt said.

"Lester is far too smart. He won't have incriminated himself enough in any way you can prove. Get Perry to turn on Tanya. Then, she'll flip on Lester in a second. Her dad will lawyer her up fast, so get any information you can out of her before Chet intervenes. She's got a big mouth, and she's full of herself." I said.

"You are definitely back to your old self. Stay away from the spiders for a while," he said.

"I'm trying." It didn't feel nearly as bad as the other one. It stung, but maybe the allergic reaction wasn't the same.

Gunnar wasted no time as he followed the ambulance to the hospital.

Dr. Brimlow stared at the spider through the evidence bag. "Black widow. How are you feeling?"

"My arm is cramping." I flexed my arm and fingers. "That's about it, right now. It's not like the other one."

"Good. No allergic reaction, but this could be unpleasant. You could be sick to your stomach, fever, chills, and so on. Motrin for pain. I'll get the nurse to check your blood pressure every fifteen minutes for the next hour. If it's stable, you can go," he said.

"My blood pressure?" I asked.

"Different spider, different problems. You're healthy. As long as it doesn't spike your BP, just treat the symptoms."

"And if her BP does spike?" Gunnar asked.

"I give her some pills to control it. It'd be temporary." Dr. Brimlow nodded. "You can talk to the girls if you want. Just remember, every fifteen minutes, back here for a recheck."

"Okay," I said. "Matt brought in the victims, right?"

Brimlow nodded. "Yep, they're being treated about ten rooms down. The girls will be admitted."

"Thanks," I said.

The nurse approached the gurney parked in the hallway that I was currently occupying and wrapped a cuff around my upper arm.

"So far so good?" I asked.

"A tiny bit high, but you've had a stressful day. Don't run a marathon or anything. See you in fifteen," she said.

I gave her a smile.

"You okay?" Gunnar asked.

"This is crazy." I extended my arm, and it trembled slightly.

"Ask your angel friends to heal you," he suggested.

"That's selfish," I said.

"What else does your guardian angel have to do? Do they cover more than one person?" he asked.

I shook my head. Gunnar did have a point. "Then, why isn't everyone in this hospital cured in an instant by their angel?"

"Fair point. Maybe you'll get some healing powers of your own?" Gunnar asked.

"Seems greedy to want more powers," I said.

He shrugged. "If the bad guys keep attacking your health, you need to adapt. If they get more and stronger powers, you need to work on that, too. Or at least try to."

I sat quietly on the bed and focused on my arm. I tried imagining the venom being neutralized by my own blood so it was harmless. I closed my eyes and visualized the venom as black droplets in my red blood. At first, the black spots seemed to be mixing with the blood and weakening it. I flipped the picture and made the blood that belonged in my body attack the black venom and take it over. It was a type of containment. That's when I felt the cramping stop. I could relax my arm and bend it without pain. I flexed my fingers without ache. I refocused and had my blood pushing the venom to my skin surface and out like sweat. That might not be how the body worked, but the visual worked for me.

We all have free will, and I willed my body to reject the venom. What else was possible for me to do if I just focused a little more?

Taking a few deep breaths, I looked at the bite itself. "Like I was never bitten," I said softly, willing the evidence to disappear.

My body felt better, but the red circle and fang marks remained.

"I tried." I shrugged.

Gunnar sighed. "Worth a shot. I've seen you do some weird crap."

"Yeah. The cramping stopped, but that might just be time." I looked at the clock. "No point in leaving, yet."

The nurse popped by a few minutes later and checked on me. "Good. No change. You might want to get some water and walk around a bit so we see if it shoots with activity. The venom is working its way through your body."

"Okay." I headed over to the series of ER rooms along the wall. I found Terry and Soli reuniting with their moms. Thankfully, their ordeal had been much shorter with less drugs ingested, so the girls were much more coherent and cognizant.

"That's her. That lady found us," Soli said.

"Thank you so much!" The first woman ran out of her ER room into the hall and hugged me tight.

"Gracias." The other woman embraced me, as well.

"Sure. How are they?" I asked.

Brimlow waved me farther into the room and a seat to update me. "Fine. They only got a few doses of the drug. Heroin can be addicting from dose one, but neither seems to be having the urge for more."

"It was a rush. Weird." Terry shook her head.

"But it'll just make you sick and dependent. He had the other girls for like a week. They had a much harder time detoxing." Brimlow tapped some notes into the computer. "You two ladies will get a room overnight for monitoring. If you're stable for twenty-four hours, then you can go home. Drink water, and we'll get you some trays of food soon."

The doc left, and I felt awkward. I got up and wandered until I spotted Matt. He stepped out of the room with the girls.

Matt cleared his throat. "You okay?" he asked.

I nodded. "Fine. What's new with you?"

"They've confirmed it was the Tanya whose father owned the bar who set them up. I checked with Kimmie, and she confirmed that was the friend who arranged their ride, as well. I'm waiting on a judge to sign a warrant."

"Did you get a statement from Perry?" I asked.

"Not yet. He's being held in an interrogation room for me, but he needs to calm down. The guy was nuts when they arrested him. We'll see if he's on drugs. Let him sweat a bit more. I'm heading there, now. By then, I should be able to pick up Tanya."

"What if he used his one phone call to warn Tanya?" I asked.

"I've got a squad on her. If she tries to flee school, they'll pick her up. They'll follow her home. I know what I'm doing." He chuckled.

"Sorry. I've been fuzzy and off for so long I'm finally feeling like I can be useful. I'm overdoing it." I looked for the clock. "I have to go have my BP checked, again."

"Fun. You look a lot better than the last spider bite," Matt said.

I nodded and wandered back to my little bed in the hallway. "Is the ER always so busy?"

Gunnar shrugged. "Big city."

I met the nurse at my spot.

"Let's see how you're doing," she said.

This time she took my BP, my temperature, and pulse. "All normal." She frowned and clipped an oxygen monitor on my finger.

"Normal is bad?" I asked.

"No, just really good. Your oxygen is good, too. You fought off that black widow amazingly. I'll grab your discharge papers and instructions. Come back if you feel sick, but you seem fine," the nurse said.

"Okay, thanks." I wasn't sure exactly what to do. My presence would not help dealing with Tanya, so I decided to go home and rest.

"So, I'm officially hired?" Gunnar asked.

"Of course, I thought we covered that." I said.

"What do we do, now?" he asked.

"Rest. Something will come up tomorrow or the next day," I said.

Chapter Seventeen

A few days later, I was fine. The spider bite healed quickly. Tanya and Perry were both charged with enough crimes to put them away for a while. Greg and I worked up preliminary notes for the crazy idea to help people. Gunnar learned his way around the mansion, met the resident ghosts and picked out the company car he wanted.

Tanya, on the other hand, refused to give up. Her father had called me. Her lawyer had called me.

When my phone rang and it was Matt, I knew he was joining the club.

"Hi, Matt, what's up?" I asked.

"This girl is a menace," he said.

"I'm shocked. After all, she did just to try and get back at me... There is a special place in hell waiting for her." I rolled my eyes. Part of me knew I should try and redeem her, but right now, that girl wasn't listening. There had to be an opening...a glimmer of wanting to change for someone to listen.

"Every cellmate she has is screaming all night. They can't prove Tanya did anything, but the girls swear she's giving them night terrors. She's threatening everyone," Matt said.

"Sounds like more charges to me," I replied.

"Yeah, I know. She keeps on saying she wants to see you. That she'll behave if she can only talk to you," Matt said.

"You don't actually believe that?" I asked.

"No, but we record all the visits. She might confess to something else if you get her worked up enough. I want everything I can get on this girl. She's a danger," Matt said.

"I don't want to see her," I said.

"I swear, you can use the phones, and there will be bulletproof glass between you two," he replied.

"Girls like her don't need a gun. But no one else will set her off quite like I do. That's not flattering. Fine. I'll visit but just once. Don't try this, again, later on," I warned.

"Nope, now is when we need info. She's going to try to plea deal out. Waive a jury trial and try to get sympathy with a judge. Her dad isn't poor, so the lawyer is good," he said.

"Okay, fine. When can I come down and get this over with?" I asked.

"Visiting hours start at two. Hit the road, and you'll be here in time. I'll put your name on the list," Matt said.

"Okay, fine. See ya," I said.

"You're really going?" Greg commented, considering he'd listened in on the entire conversation.

I shrugged. "If it can possibly add to her charges, it's worth it. I know the courts will go easy on her. Poor little rich girl. She doesn't know better. Blah blah. Feel like driving, Gunnar?" I asked.

"I can take you," Greg offered.

"No, I'm going stir crazy," Gunnar insisted.

After a dull drive, I signed in to visit, was searched, and put in a room. I expected to be one of many visitors in a big room. Maybe juvie was different? Maybe Tanya was under special restrictions? It didn't matter in the long run, but I felt oddly alone.

I sat and waited. The glass was there, but Tanya and I didn't need contact to do damage. I wouldn't hurt her; she needed to be punished by the state. I just didn't like meeting with her. Giving in to her demands only encouraged her. Seeing her gave her a chance to try and get revenge.

The door opened, and she walked out wearing a hideous jumpsuit. Her hair was pulled back in a ponytail. She glared at me.

Finally, she sat and picked up the phone handset.

I picked up mine.

"Well, I'm here," I said.

I braced myself for Tanya's sort of venom. Cursing and blame. Or maybe she'd try tears and think she could pretend to have learned her lesson well enough.

"You have to interview me. I want an insanity plea," she said seriously.

I suppressed a laugh. Not much about this case was worth laughing over, but this girl really needed to grow up before she threw her powers around, again. I wondered if she'd traded her soul for them. There were other ways, but she was way out of her league.

"I can't diagnose you. Tanya. Whether I can prove it or not, you hired a man to help you put a curse on me. He set his zombie out to kill me. That stuff is hard to prosecute, but what you did to those girls isn't. What the hell was Perry doing with them, really?" I asked.

"I don't know. That was all him. It was just payment to get help from Lester. I was brainwashed by these black magic practitioners. You have to believe me, I'm a victim here. I should've listened to you and the Ghost Tamers. You guys were good," she said and rolled her eyes.

I smirked. "Your lawyer has you well-rehearsed. Did you and Perry give statements on Lester?" I asked.

She shrugged. "I can't really prove anything. Perry is a student of his and spent more real time with him. He was the go-between. I never met the master in person. I paid in teenage youth that Perry sucked from me. I'm glad the girls are okay. They said they wouldn't really be harmed."

"Not harmed? They were drugged for days. Not fed, just given liquor. The first three are still in the hospital. You tried to kill me. So, you did intend harm," I said.

"I knew I wouldn't and couldn't kill you. You're too powerful. But you wouldn't teach me how to get powers." She glared at me.

"You can't get my powers by dark magic or manipulation. You were feeding off of demonic powers at your dad's bar and playing with pretty evil ghosts. That's dangerous. Didn't your dad ever take you to church?" I asked.

She laughed. "My dad loves money and liquor. That's why he runs a bar. He acts like he cares about me when people bring it up, but I do what I want. He looks the other way. But he wouldn't give me enough money to buy the services. But lending them some girls for a bit didn't seem like a big deal."

"And your dad believes you're a victim of Lester." I couldn't totally blame the kid when the father was so uninvolved.

"He won't blame me. That'd mean he has to spend time on me and try to fix me. He'd rather I stay in here to be corrected or a mental health facility. Better a place with crazies than criminals," Tanya said.

"You'll mess with those girls more. You're going to hurt people. The more freedom you get, the worse it'll be." I wasn't going to let her off the hook.

"I don't hurt people who don't hurt me usually," she whined. "You took away my fun at the bar. You took away the teachers I'd attracted on my own."

"Teachers? A demon and his captive ghosts are not teachers. You need to learn right from wrong. Giving in to evil means you work for them. They're your masters, not your teachers. Tanya, you are lucky we got you away from Perry and Lester. There are good mentors out there, but you won't get results fast enough to keep you happy. You'd have to work, not just buy things."

"That's how my dad always gets everything. Buys off people or blackmail." She shrugged.

For a moment, I was reminded she was a young teen. Her experience and view of the world was narrow, even with the Internet and social media—she still only had what her limited life lessons had taught her.

"Help me. I'm not violent. I'm not tough. Those girls will beat me up and stuff. They fight. Some of them killed their boyfriends. I want to be safe," she pleaded.

"A mental health ward won't be much better. It's the facility's job to keep you safe. You tell them you're in for messing with Hoodoo and getting girls kidnapped, you'll scare off the bad girls," I said.

"No, I've met a bunch of them in juvie here. Plenty of these girls do Voodoo and curses. They have family training. And their family could do a lot worse to me. One girl wanted me to be her girlfriend for protection. I need out," she said.

"I don't have the ability to do that, even if I wanted to. Which I don't. You need to be punished. You need to learn other people's safety and lives matter. We're not your entertainment. We're not your playthings."

"I do know that. Now. I hate what I did. Maybe I just resent not having a mom around," she said.

"Oh, wow. You're going to throw every Hail Mary pass in the world at the judge?" I asked.

"I don't know what that means, but I'll try anything to get out or get a better deal. Can you at least be a character witness?" she asked.

"Absolutely," I said.

"Really?" She smiled.

"Against you, yes. The judge needs to know why you need to be locked up."

"No!" she screamed.

"Don't worry, you'll find plenty of demons and ghosts in jail," I said. Unfortunately, I was afraid that was true, and she'd only grow in her evil powers. "But you'll also find people with more powers than you. Be careful what enemies and friends you make."

"No, please! I'll try to be good. Help me," she shrieked.

I hung up the phone. She wasn't ready for real change. She needed to let go of the desire for power before she understood the meaning behind true power and control.

I walked away as security came in and took her out. She struggled and fought them. I felt sorry for the staff there, but they had restraints and solitary lockdown.

Chapter Eighteen

The Ghost Tamers were royally pissed about the development with their former case because I hadn't informed them. Steve breaking up with me didn't help, but they were all about the show. They'd gone back to the bar with Greg and cleared it out, just in case Tanya had brought back any bad things to fester. Luckily, I'd managed to dodge any direct involvement with them. I had tried working with a TV show and a different team, but it didn't work. I wasn't one for broadcasting my cases.

"The Ghost Tamers hate me?" I asked.

Greg smiled. "Steve is still bitter, but he wasn't strong enough for you. That group is good at what they do, but the show comes first. Chet didn't want to talk to them. You won't do another interview. Chet let them film us checking out the bar to make sure it was safe and demon-free, but he wasn't thrilled about bringing you back."

"He doesn't know I'm here?" I asked.

"He's off tonight, and the assistant manager wanted to know the place was clear. You're the strongest demon and ghost detector we have. We're fine," he said.

"Steve was weird. I thought he was laid back enough to deal with my weird life, but he needed to be invited in and didn't really fit. I think he was jealous of you and then Gunnar." I sipped my coffee.

Greg laughed. "Jealous of me? Hardly. Gunnar? That first night in the ER, he did have on a lot of body glitter."

"Bachelorette party traditions are important. I wonder how that girl is doing?" I mulled.

"Better than you with a second spider bite," he replied.

I waved it off. "This one was nothing. The first one? I don't know if it was the curse or if I'm really allergic to that spider so it was worse. Better than being bitten by a poisonous snake from around here."

"Very true. Gunnar thought you might have healed yourself a bit. Did it work?" Greg asked.

I shook my head. "I don't think so. He suggested I try. It's still got a bit of a scab." I pulled up my sleeve and showed him.

"No rush to push for new powers. I can see you getting more intense," he said.

"The battle is getting worse. Demons. Teenage girls trying to kill and curse me. Lester. I don't even know what Lester is," I said.

"I need to have a sit down with this guy," Greg said.

"He has a power trip. He manipulates people. I don't know what he was sucking all this energy for. I mean, my curse was in place. What did he need those teens' energy for?" I asked.

"Payment, it sounds like." He shrugged.

"Collecting energy. How do you store that? Why would he need it?" I wanted to pretend that Lester didn't exist, but he did. He was out there, and he knew me.

"It seemed like he was afraid of you," Greg said.

"No, not afraid. He respected my power. It's more like don't step on his toes or turf and he won't come after me. How can I not go after him?" I asked.

"You can't prove anything, now. Unless you can put him behind bars, you're only antagonizing him. Matt is going to keep an eye on the guy. His record is clean. Don't get into a supernatural battle, because that won't end," Greg said.

"Did Gran ever face this sort of thing?" I asked.

"Demons and bad people, sure. Her powers didn't go past visions and psychic-type work. You can move things with your mind. That power will grow, and who knows, you might develop some healing. The more you're pushed, the stronger you'll get." Greg nodded.

"I'm not sure that's what I want. I don't want you, Ivy, or Gunnar in danger," I said.

"Gunnar is a good choice. He can handle himself. He needs to start carrying a gun—you do, too. Lester is a human. If he threatens you or attacks you, you can defend yourself. Don't forget he's as mortal as you are," Greg said.

"I just don't know how extreme his powers are," I admitted.

"You will. Just don't obsess about him. He's not worth it, and he's not the only dangerous force in New Orleans," Greg said.

"So, should we walk this place? I don't think anything is hiding here. It feels like you cleared out the place, again," I said.

"Can't hurt to check the back and the top floors," Greg said.

I nodded and headed for the familiar staircase. Before, there had been ghosts trapped and a demon playing with humans. It felt much lighter, but we needed to look in every nook and cranny, just in case.

That night, I felt like I was being watched. I looked at the sleeping cat sprawled on her back. Occasionally, her paw stretched up, but she wasn't stalking me.

I turned and saw my angel, Gran, and three others.

"Hi. So nice of you to knock." I cleared my throat and sat up.

"We've been expecting you to come for a visit. Since meeting Lester," Gran said.

I rubbed my eyes then grabbed the bottle of water on my nightstand. The cat woke up and stared at my guests. She hissed.

"No, they're okay." I stroked Tish.

She bounded down to the floor and sniffed them. She pawed at my angel and then darted from the room.

Gran shrugged.

"Missy and Noah don't bother her," I said. "Why would I visit because of Lester?"

"He's worrying you," Gran said.

"I'd be a fool if he didn't worry me. He's strong and not in a good way. Who are they?" I asked

The other entities sort of looked like angels but bigger. Scarier looking.

"Warriors," my angel said. "You've been assigned additional protection."

"Because of Lester?" I asked.

"And Tanya. That girl is bad and power hungry," Gran said.

"Gran, if you pulled strings for this, I'm fine. Really," I said.

"No one can pull strings for this. You're taking on new levels of fighting evil. You will have more protection and more powers. Be grateful," my angel said.

"I am. So, did I heal my spider bite or not?" I asked.

"Mostly. You neutralized the venom, which is what you asked for. The bite heals on its own. But that's smart," she said.

"I'm smart? I just want to make sure I heard that right." I teased my angel.

"You are smart in that you don't ask for the world. You don't expect magical fixes. Which is why you are being trusted with bigger problems and more help. Don't abuse it," she said.

I looked at Gran. "How bad is this?"

"I'm very proud of you," she said.

"Oh, hell." I sat back on the pillows. "Is Eddie doing better?"

"She has no interest," said one of the warrior angels.

"I don't need you, now. I'm fine. What are your names?" I asked.

They stood silent.

"Names don't matter," Gran said.

"To humans, they do. How can I call for their help if they won't tell me their names?" I asked.

"They will always be with you until they are reassigned. But your work will not be over quickly. Get used to them," my angel said.

"Okay. Moe, Larry, and Curly. When I call for The Three Stooges, that's you. Unless there is evil or something bad in my bedroom, you stay out. I like my privacy. You can find an empty room and make it your space." I nodded.

"You don't order them, De," Gran said.

"Why not? They look male; I don't want strange men lurking around my bedroom. She's enough. If she calls for their help, fine. They can pick rooms or just roam the halls, guarding my house. I don't care. As long as I know how to call for them when I need them," I said.

"They will just know," my angel said.

"Okay. So, what about Lester?" I asked.

"He's dangerous," Gran said.

"I realize that. I don't have anything to put him in jail." I shrugged.

"He's too smart for that. You must keep the peace, for now," the angel said.

"The peace?" I asked.

"His evil is leveled by your good. He didn't try to intimidate you or frighten you because he felt your power matched his. A fight would lead to you both being exhausted and no one winning. You have more friends. He has minions, but he can't trust they won't turn on him. So, he's waiting for you to make a move. To indicate if you'll fight him or let the peace stand," Amy said.

I rubbed the back of my neck. "This is like Game of Thrones crap. Do we negotiate or fight?"

"Neither. You stalemate, for now. Grow your numbers. Grow your powers. Hide your angels.

Show no fear, but you must show him you don't fear him and you will let the peace remain as long as he does not harm innocents," Gran said.

"What about Greg's crazy idea for helping everyone? It might drain some resources," I said.

Amy and Gran shared a look.

"What? It's not my money. I don't mind living off it for what I need, but I'm not digging into the principal and spending millions without your okay. This would cost that at least. It's a huge undertaking," I said.

"And it could help thousands of people at once. People minorly afflicted with things. It's good work," Gran said.

"And a good cover for growing your powers and learning about the opposition. Lester and his crew will think you're busy helping launch this huge project. He might try to attack it or sabotage it a bit for fun, but he lacks your financial resources," Amy added.

"Another reason he's not coming at you directly. You're rich. You live in the Garden District. Your family is old money and well-known here. You have friends and respect in the community. He is a loner who craves power, not people. He'll collect souls to keep the demons happy, but it's a toll he pays," Gran said.

"So, go ahead with that rehab thing. What about Brimlow? Is he really good? I might need his help," I said.

"He is good. Only a truly good soul could share their body with the Angel of Death. He doesn't fully remember it, but the more he's around you, the more he will believe the memories he has from his coma," my angel explained.

"And Steve. Why do I keep picking the wrong guys?" I asked.

Gran nodded, and my angel vanished.

"Oh, she's not interested in my personal life." I chuckled.

"You'll take it better from me." Gran sat on the edge of the bed. "Steve was safe. You aren't meant for a safe and easy love. The right man will push you. Challenge you in good ways."

"Don't tell me it's Greg. I can't deal with the former priest thing," I said.

"No, it's not Greg. You haven't met him, yet. No clues. No hints. You can always choose to reject someone if you don't want the challenge. That's free will, and sometimes, it backfires," she said.

"I'll live either way. I just hope those angels don't stir up Lester and his friends. If he can sense them." I wanted to go back to sleep and not think about any of this mess.

"I wouldn't worry about that. When he finds out, he finds out. You don't control the time or the place."

"Great, thanks for the information. Maybe I should get some sleep?" I said.

"Of course, get your rest." Gran disappeared.

Chapter Nineteen

Lester was nagging in my brain, and since the late-night visit from my odd angel crew, I knew I had to pay my new nemesis a visit. He'd manipulated and used people. Was Tanya some pawn to get to me? I had no idea, but Lester wasn't some small-time nothing peddling crystals to tourists. He had powers, and powers could be used for good and for evil.

"You're sure?" Gunnar asked as he parked in front of the creepy old house.

He loved his new shiny red SUV with lots of buttons, but even that didn't make him happy to do this job.

"I need to pay him a visit. You just hang by the door and watch my back," I said.

"Done. But I'm only good for human attacks. I don't have any proton guns like Ghostbusters." He reached behind him and checked his gun.

"I've got that covered." I exited the car and headed through the front door, this time.

The zombie was in the front area of the shop. His eyes widened when he recognized me.

"Tom, you don't need to be afraid of me. I can help you live a normal life. Don't you want that?" I asked.

He didn't answer. Had he truly given up all his free will? What was this world coming to?"

"Get your master for me," I demanded.

He went to the back without a word.

"That guy needs help," Gunnar said.

"I tried." I held up my hand. One step at a time.

"Deanna, how kind of you to call," Lester said in a syrupy sweet tone.

"I felt I needed to stop by now that you've lost two of your students. Too bad I can't find enough proof to put this one in prison." I gestured to his minion.

The zombie darted to hide out of sight.

"I thought you'd want me, not him," Lester said.

"I really don't have enough proof on you either. And you know that. You need to stop attacking young girls," I said.

"I did nothing." Lester smiled.

"I've heard that before. But I'm watching you. You won't get away with what you've been doing. If I can't find a legal way, I'll find another way to stop you. The law works to an extent, but we're not limited. Are we?" I asked.

Lester picked up a pentagram. "You're too good to start a war with me. Keep that bodyguard of yours on a leash. If he hits me, again, I will prosecute. The law entertains and keeps the powerless out of our way."

"That won't happen, again, unless you or your zombie make a move on us. I don't want war. I want peace, which means you behaving well enough that I don't have to bother with you. Either one of us can start the war, but you can keep it from happening," I said.

"Please. You're not up for it. Not yet. You're helping the police. You're wasting your time on a life or two, here or there. This game is so much bigger than one silly police case. The world is falling apart. So much energy and time wasted for some girls who'll be nothing. You're falling for the distractions." Lester smirked.

"You admit distracting me by hurting young girls? Stop hurting innocents, and we can keep the peace," I said.

"I admit nothing. I'm not what you have to worry about. There are much bigger evil purveyors and monsters than me. They love watching you spin your wheels over a few people while they are laying bigger traps. Big evil is spreading."

"I've handled demons before. Don't think I'm small time just because I care about every soul. That's the difference between good and evil. You don't care what happens to Perry or Tanya. They served some purpose for you, and even if you didn't get everything you wanted, you're not going to jail. Pretty nice deal," I said.

"You're welcome to join me. It's a lot more fun on the dark side," he replied.

I laughed. "No deal. I've seen what your kind of deals gets people in the end. You'll be sorry, Lester. You'll be asking me for help," I said.

"Really?" He tossed the pentagram on the floor in front of me.

A large shadow-type creature appeared, big enough to be the Hulk. Was he mist or solid? I couldn't see through him. The cold, growling, and evil demon was far too close to me, now. Lester had summoned a demon on command. He had powers, but I pushed away any fear. He wanted me to run.

Gunnar drew his weapon, but I waved my hand. The demon slammed into the back of the house and the zombie scrambled out the back door. The creature wasn't made of mist; I could impact him. I grinned. Hurting human bad guys was frowned on; I could get in trouble for that. But no one said I couldn't pound on a demon or two.

The demon tried to pursue the zombie, for some reason. Maybe he was trying to get away with me? Either way, I held him with my mind, the same way I'd isolated the venom in my own blood. If I believed I had the power and control, apparently, I did. A demon more than three times my size raged against my powers.

"What are you going to do with him, now, Deanna? You caught the demon. You have the monster by its toe, but what do to with it?" Lester asked.

I could call my angels, but I didn't want to tip my hand. Giving away all my powers and tricks wasn't necessary. Some things were best when handled simply. The demon was powerful and scary, but I couldn't show any hint of fear. I had to toss him away like a gnat or a new spider bite.

The spider bites kept ringing in my memory. I looked at the pentagram on the floor and the lines blurred in my mind to make a spider.

"You like spiders, Lester?" I asked.

"You're holding a demon, and you want to talk about spiders?" Lester chuckled.

"You're right. First things first. Death!" I shouted.

"What?" Lester laughed.

"I summon the Angel of Death to return this demon to the depths of Hell where it belongs," I said firmly.

"Death obeys you?" Lester mocked.

The lady with dreads showed up. "Well, dis is a treat. It's not every day I get a demon hand-delivered. You earned yerself a few more free passes, girl."

Lester stared at her, his jaw slack.

"Boo!" she said to him. "My real appearance would kill you both. So, I borrow human bodies when I have to deal wid you creatures."

"He's all yours," I said.

"Put it back in dat medallion. I don't want to mess up my hair fightin' with dat ting," she ordered.

It was a test of my abilities. I focused and contained the demon's energy, pushing him into the tiny metal object. I tuned out everything else and concentrated on controlling that demon, just like I'd contained that black widow venom. He was sealed up nicely in seconds.

Death picked it up. "Good. Thanks. Stay off my list." She smiled and vanished.

Lester gritted his teeth. "You summon high-level angels?"

"The highest level. And you summon demons. Our war will be a draw, for now. Not worth the waste of our time and energy, agreed?" I asked.

He nodded reluctantly.

"Any move made on me or my friends or innocents, and I will step in. I will fight you and all your little zombie and demon minions if I have to. I'll take them out like a bug zapper. That's the nice thing about evil supernatural creatures—I don't have to explain them to the cops," I said.

"Some students go bad. I'm not responsible for their crimes. I simply sell things and teach things. There are hundreds, if not thousands, of shops just like mine all over New Orleans. I might have to report you for harassing me," Lester said.

"Oh, now, that's a baby move. You just said you were in the big game, and now, you're going to bite at my ankles? I've got the cops in my pocket already. And all those other shops out there, they're not just like yours. Your shop is much more remote than the others. I wonder why?" I asked.

"I like my privacy. I like serious students and buyers. I don't want tourists. And so much is done online. I have a great Web presence. I sell tons online. Do you?" he asked.

"I'm not trying to sell anything or attract a following. Don't start up some black church or cult. I've already had to shut one of those down," I replied.

"Interesting. Well, I hope you have more than Death and that male model over there to protect you. Death can only take who is named on the list. Demons are already residents of Hell, so that's a technicality. If it's not my time, no matter how bad I am, Death can't take me." He shrugged.

Death wasn't the scariest thing he should worry about, but it had impressed Lester. "Did you sell your soul to a devil? Is that why you're not worried about Death?" I taunted him. "Death is an old friend, not my big guns. You're not worth pulling out my big guns, Lester. Stalemate, like I said."

Lester glared at me. "I'll still die when I die. The game is bigger than you and me."

"Much bigger. I'm in no rush to play that game. Now, about the spiders." I leaned on his display case. "You have a lot of spider designs."

"Trinkets for tourists," he said.

"Sign says true believers only," Gunnar said.

"Did you set spiders on me?" I asked Lester.

"That's crazy. Spiders can't kill you. Unless it was a swarm or something. You're paranoid. Maybe you're afraid of me?" He stood a bit taller.

"Nah, I learned how to cure myself of venomous attacks. Pretty easy, actually. But I wouldn't try that, again." I turned and nodded to Gunnar.

He opened the door, and we left.

Chapter Twenty

Mardi Gras is a long day. Actually, it's more of a weeklong party with tourists packing the streets and drinking. The club did a bang-up business normally, but the whole of New Orleans cleaned up at Mardi Gras. Our party was invitation-only, but Gunnar had invited some of his hot stripper friends, so we were an even hotter ticket than normal.

Ivy was judging the wet tighty-whitey contest that I hadn't sanctioned, but she knew how to please a crowd. Gunnar was keeping an eye on the door. Things had been calm and quiet. Tanya got her day before the judge and tried her pleas of mental illness. She was remanded to juvie until age eighteen, and if she needed mental care, she'd get it there.

Lester had been quiet, and Chet, as well. Greg and I had a plan and a potential building to tour. We'd had a few cases but nothing criminal, yet, so it was relaxing.

A man with a stack of boxes on a dolly came to the door.

Gunnar went and handled it. Honestly, having him around was great. The police skills and open mind were the perfect mix. Plus, he was gay, so no teasing of me robbing the cradle or whatever.

"Delivery," Gunnar said. He set a box on the bar.

I could smell what they were. "Paczki!" I said.

I opened the box and grabbed one. "These are so good."

I took a bite.

"I don't know what that word is. Do you just eat what random people send you without asking who?" Gunnar asked.

"These? Yes. The risk is worth it," I said with my mouth full. "Try one."

The boxes were piled on the bar. I savored the Polish masterpiece so beloved in Chicago. "So much better than a plastic baby in a cake."

Gunnar grabbed one and took a bite. "Like a Bismarck but... Damn, that's good."

"It's the dough. Little Polish ladies have handed down the recipe for decades. Luckily, Chicago has the biggest Polish population outside of Warsaw." I kissed the pastry.

Greg came over. "Those donuts things?"

"Yep. Who sent them, Gunnar?" I asked.

He handed me a card.

I opened it. De, I know you're missing these. Enjoy! Frankie...P.S. Look up.

I looked up, and my brother was at the door.

I ran around the bar and threw my arms around him. "What are you doing here?"

"I love Chicago as much as you do, but everywhere I look—I see Eddie. I got depressed. Believe it or not, I went to a shrink. He suggested I get a change of scenery for a bit."

"Like a vacation?" Ivy rushed up and hugged him

Greg was right behind and shook Frankie's hand.

"Vacation or longer. I started looking for jobs, but I saw the pastry and decided to surprise you. Hope you don't mind a squatter," he said.

"I've got the room. Thanks for the pastries!" I turned and grabbed one more before the crowd ate them all.

"Got luggage?" Gunnar asked.

"It's in the car. That is a long drive," Frankie said.

"Frankie, my new assistant Gunnar. Gunnar, my brother Frankie," I introduced them.

"Hi, another roomie?" Frankie asked.

"No, he has his own place." I shrugged.

"But Ivy and Greg still live with you?" Frankie asked.

"Yeah. Is it weird?" I asked.

"No, it's like a fire station where everyone is on hand. That's why I thought you'd have your assistant in house, too," Frankie said.

"I didn't know room and board was an option." Gunnar winked. "Let's get you a drink."

Ivy followed along.

"The house gets fuller," Greg said.

"I don't know if Gunnar would or should move in. He's young. We're not exactly a

201

swinging time at the mansion. I can't believe Frankie came down." I hopped up on a bar stool and ordered a diet soda from the bartender.

"It's good to see you smile. Most people are happy on Mardi Gras." Greg grabbed a pastry.

"I was happy enough today," I said.

"You've been focused and even. Not happy," he said.

I shrugged. "I have a lot of my mind and trying to deal and plan with the future. Sometimes, I rush too fast and screw it up. Or I second guess and overthink things. I'm trying to trust my gut, but it seemed like something was missing. I thought it was Eddie because I haven't seen him in so long."

"At least you get to spend some more time with your other brother." Greg bit into the pastry.

"Good, right?" I asked.

He nodded and took another bite.

"He better not be sick," I said softly.

I spotted Gran in the corner, shaking her head at me. Then, I knew he was safe, and I was free from worry—for now.

The party went on, and finally, Mary Lou showed up about an hour after my brother did.

"Sorry I'm so late. The traffic. The family crap." She hugged me and nodded to Greg. He'd been one of her many affairs, but it's something we never discussed.

"My brother is here," I said.

"Eddie made it to Heaven, and he visited? That's so great!" Mary Lou said.

"No, my other brother. Frankie. He got a little down up in Chicago and is going to spend some time here in New Orleans with me," I said. I craned my neck, trying to find him in the crowd.

"That's so great. How are your parents doing?" Mary Lou asked.

"Fine. They don't like change. Dad is doing better about his health, now that Mom is the only one nagging him at home. Men and their egos. He'd fight when the kids were around, like he had to show he was in charge. It's his health. He should do the right thing no matter what anyone says."

"He should do it himself. Not make your mother set up his pills and cook healthy food," Mary Lou said.

"When did you turn feminist?" Greg asked.

"Well, it's his health. It's not your mother's job. She'll kill herself taking care of everyone else, and then, he'll be alone, anyway." Mary Lou grinned.

"Where's Frankie? Greg, can you see?" I asked.

He was several inches taller than me, and he stood tall to get a better look. "Dancing."

"Open-minded brother of yours, dancing in a gay club to a slow song," Mary Lou said.

"Dancing with who?" I asked.

Greg smiled.

"No," I said.

He shrugged. "Go look if you don't believe me."

I slipped through the crowd and found my brother slow dancing with Ivy.

Turning before they saw me, I headed back to the bar. "Rum and Diet Coke," I said.

"Told you," Greg said.

"When did that happen?" I asked.

"Men work fast," Mary Lou said.

"Ivy works faster," Greg said.

"I never thought about why Frankie didn't bring girls home much. He always had girls after him. Eddie was technically cuter and got more attention. I just thought he was private." I downed the drink.

"Would you rather it was Gunnar?" Greg asked.

"Rather what was me?" Gunnar asked as he slid up to the bar.

"Dancing with my brother," I said.

"Is he gay? Nice." Gunnar nodded.

"He's dancing with Ivy," I said.

Gunnar pondered that for a moment. "No, I'm not down for that cat fight. She can have him."

"He's my brother, not a piece of meat," I said.

"Honey, it's a gay bar, and he's put himself on the menu. Deal," Gunnar said.

"Nice back talk from my assistant," I said.

"I tell you the truth. You said no secrets, no lies, and I'm following the rules. Just find yourself a hotter guy." Gunnar shrugged.

"It's not a competition. It's just new information. No wonder he came down here," I said.

Greg laughed. "Got it. The relocation was about getting away from potentially judgmental parents and to the sister who owns a gay drag club. The guy is smart."

I nodded. "Hey, Gunnar, want to move in to the mansion?"

"For real? I was just kidding," he said.

"No, for real. If I need to go out on late-night calls or get a vision, it'll be easier when you're down the hall. And if my brother and Ivy become a real thing under my roof—" I paused.

"They're dancing. Don't jump to happily ever after so fast," Greg said.

"I know, I know. but if it's a thing... My best friend and my brother. I might need Gunnar to pull me off of strangling one or both of them someday. Greg, you're just not as young as you used to be," I teased.

"And Ivy is my cousin. I'll always take her side," he said honestly.

"Exactly. Gunnar is the non-related neutral party to keep things sane," I said.

Gunnar nodded. "Same salary?"

"Yep, now, you get room and board." I shrugged.

"Done. I can help my mom out more. Nice place. I can bring guys over?" he asked.

"Yeah, just no loud parties or anything without prior approval. Deal?" I asked.

"Done." He shook my hand. "I can go cut in on them, if you want."

"No, don't do it for me. If you want to make that a three-way mess, I'm really going to stay out of it." I added another splash of rum to my drink.

"Fine. Would you like to dance?" Gunnar asked Mary Lou.

"Why not?" she said.

Greg offered me his hand. "What are old friends for?"

I took his hand. Someday, the right guy would show up, but for now, I had my friends and my brother. And a crazy team of angels that were huddled in the corner, watching us weird humans enjoy life. Did they disapprove? Were they jealous? I didn't know.

One thing I knew for sure, no one was going to shoot at my club tonight.

Epilogue

M att was riding high; he'd gotten all the girls back alive, and two people in jail for it. Perry took a plea in the end. Tanya had turned on him as much as he'd turned on her. He'd dragged me out to lunch to celebrate Perry's deal being inked. It meant one less trial.

It was a funky little place on the edge of the French Quarter. Half of the menu was actually Cajun, and my French sucked, so I ordered a burger and fries like Matt.

"Too bad we couldn't be there for Tanya's sentencing," I said.

"I was at a crime scene. Murder trumps sentencing. Plus, juvie courts tend to be very closed, I'd have had to jump through a lot of hoops to get you in for that. Even with you testifying, they don't want a big crowd. Kids screw up, and they don't want to make it a big public spectacle. She's locked up until eighteen and that's about all you can ask. Minors get away with a lot because the courts hope they'll learn and rehab in juvie rather than keep on a bad path. She was way too young to be considered to be charged as an adult. Girls usually have to be at least seventeen before they want to push them to adult prison," Matt said.

"Either way, she's in a great place to grow her evil powers. So is Perry, for that matter," I said.

"Perry only got five years. He didn't harm the girls beyond tying them up. His lawyer made a good argument that he was influenced by another." Matt sighed and dug into his burger.

"Too bad they couldn't get Perry to flip on Lester," I said.

"Nah, they tried. But Perry's lawyer threatened to take it to trial. Have a psych eval that could prove Perry was mentally challenged, and he'd get a mental health lockup. The court didn't want that. Deals get cut all the time," Matt replied.

"Yeah, the system is what it is. We did our best. At least they're locked up for a while. I did pay Lester a visit, so he knows we're keeping an eye on him. He's into some dark stuff, but he's way too smart to get caught." I dunked a fry in some ketchup.

"We've got him on our list. A patrol rolls by there every other day or so," Matt said.

"That's nice but won't stop what he's doing. He's still got that zombie. Maybe he's making more of them. I don't know if he's starting a cult or just brainwashing a select few to take the fall for his illegal stuff. You're better off tailing the zombies. You can get Tom for driving a stolen car. We don't need him to find his master, anymore. Before we had a reason to leave him on the loose, but now, if you want to have him picked up." I shrugged.

Matt smiled. "You know I hate loose ends." He pulled out his cell phone and told whoever was on the other line to run the plates for any car in the lot of Lester's place, and if any stolen plates popped up, wait and arrest whoever got in that car.

I lifted my glass of iced tea, unsweetened—I'd never get used to tea so sweet that it hurt your teeth. Matt lifted his sweet tea, and we clinked glasses to a job well done.

"Now, is there any way you think I can get Gunnar back on the force? He's got the skills. I hate to see him playing babysitter to you," Matt said.

"Not babysitter, anymore. I admit, when I was recovering from spider bites, I needed a driver. But he's muscle. He's an extra set of hands. I had Greg for a while, and he's got so many demonic cases that he needs an assistant, too. Gunnar has the skills I need to keep me out of trouble." I smiled. "Sorry."

"It's not because he's hot?" Matt asked.

"Please, he's gay. But him being in shape and young helps. I'm not twenty, anymore. It's one thing to take on demons and ghosts but real-life criminals run and fight with their fists." I shuddered.

Matt laughed. "You are a mystery. I'm glad you're on my side, though."

"Me, too." I could never lose sight of what side I was on and why.

A few hours later, I walked into Dr. Brimlow's office in a building attached to the hospital. I'd asked him to look at the preliminary plan for the crazy undertaking. Gunnar, my new assistant, was with me out of habit more than necessity today.

"Deanna, I'm glad you could make it. I'd have come to you, but I want you to meet someone. Hello, Gunnar." Brimlow shook my hand.

Gunnar gave a quick wave.

"Oh? Who do I need to meet with?" I asked.

"First, I want to say this is amazing. It's like a dream project for anyone who has ever worked in a shelter or in the mental health system. You're incredibly generous, and it's a huge undertaking. The approvals and permits will take time, but I think you know the right people to make things happen." Brimlow was a lot more positive about things, now. Maybe he thought we were just shooting up a pipe dream before.

"Money has its advantages. I know the people who know the people, at least. But I need medical staff I can trust and that will lead with the right views and work ethic. The old ways don't always work; we're taking the best of the old and putting in some new protocols," I said.

"I agree; that's why I want you to meet Dr. LeBlanc." Brimlow led us a few doors down and gave a quick knock on the door.

"Enter," a voice replied.

"Dr. LeBlanc, Dr. Oscar and her friend are here," Brimlow said.

"Dr. Oscar?" LeBlanc studied me. He was tall but deliberately looked down his nose at me. He was hot with dark hair and eyes, but he seemed more impressed with himself than anyone. Not really the type of ally I was looking for. "PhD in psychology?"

"Yes. You're a psychiatrist?" I asked.

"Brimlow says you have psychic skills. Is that true?" he asked.

"Yes, but your specialization was just a good guess. So, you're interested in my new undertaking?" I asked.

"Brimlow asked for my opinion. You're taking on a lot. Changing the way things are done. The religious component will get you in trouble," he said.

Gunnar held up a finger. "AA and all the twelve-step programs talk about submitting to a higher power and admitting you need their help. Greg already has some nuns interested in working as nurses, aides or whatever. Most are retired nurses or schoolteachers. Some got screwed on their retirement."

"Oh, nice. Love to have them. But they have to wear the scrubs unless they work reception or counseling. No old-fashioned habits either. I don't want to trigger someone with Catholic school trauma," I said.

"I'll text Greg." Gunnar pulled out his phone.

"Nuns? You can't force religion on everyone," LeBlanc said.

"It's not force; it's staff. Patients can opt out or use their own faith, but the staff will offer all the options to all of the patients, and quiet reflective time is mandatory. Call it meditation or whatever people like best." I shrugged.

"Obviously, you're very rich and used to getting your way. That doesn't mean it'll work. All this money could go to research or current efforts," he said.

"I think you're misunderstanding me, Dr. LeBlanc. I'm looking for input from Brimlow and other medical professionals so this will work. I want the best input so we can create the best facilities. I am a trained and respected psychologist, so I'm not out of my depth as far as mental health goes. If you're not interested, that's fine. If you don't want to work with a psychic, that's fine, too. A lot of people think I need treatment." I folded my arms.

"Psychics," he scoffed as I turned to leave.

I turned back. "It is an unfortunate label. But we all get labeled. Shrink. Psychic sounds like I tell fortunes at summer carnivals next to a balloon pop booth. Visionary. Seer. Pick a word; it doesn't matter. I've helped the police save lives. I can save more this way. A place for pregnant teens hooked on drugs, and a separate facility for vets who need help with their PTSD before they get turn violent. Instead of waiting for the VA, we get them before they hurt themselves or anyone else."

"I respect your goals. I think it's a lot more than one person can bring about." LeBlanc shrugged.

I smiled. "One person with a whole lot of money hiring a lot of people to make it happen. I've already got donations for the LGBT facility, so it's paid for through the first year. We're not above taking contributions, but no one will dictate to me what can and can't be done, except the law of the land."

"The religious component will be a problem. You're a psychic. People might think your spirit guide told you to do this. You'll face huge public mocking, even in New Orleans," he said.

I rolled my eyes. "I don't have a spirit guide. I have an angel. So do you. I have ghost friends

212

and relations. And when I need approval, I go to Heaven and get it. Now, before you try to slap a straitjacket on me, I assure you—I'm not crazy."

"Really? Other than helping the police, what proof do you have? You've gotten lucky." He smirked.

I looked behind him at the diplomas on the wall. "I've got my degrees. Just like you have yours. Very impressive schooling. You must have mountains of student loan debt."

I waved my hand and all the diplomas fell on the floor.

"What the hell?" He took a step toward me.

Gunnar stood between us. "Not a good idea, man."

"I'm not violent, really. I just..." He stared back and rubbed his eyes.

"The woman in that picture isn't your birth mother." I pointed to the one framed object that remained up on the wall.

He glared at me. "How do you know that? Brimlow told you you'd meet with me, and you researched me."

"No, I never gave her your name," Brimlow said.

"No one told me about you. That woman is your stepmother. She was very good to you. Your real mother died shortly after giving birth because she went on a drug binge. You were born mildly addicted to heroin, but it doesn't seem to have affected your mind or body." He did have a nice body. Broad shoulders and strong arms. He wore a dress shirt open at the neck and suit pants. The jacket was on the coat rack.

I felt a little underdressed in jeans and a t-shirt.

"How do you know all of that?" he asked.

"Your father finished rehab and stayed clean. Married a nice woman, and lucky you had a better childhood than you might have. You get what I'm trying to do. If you have a better idea, a better way to do something, suggest it. But don't crap on something because you're anti-religion. You want an alternative for the non-religious patients, write it up. I'll consider anything legal."

"So, no medical marijuana?" Gunnar asked.

"Wrong state for it. My brother used it a bit when he had really harsh chemo side effects. It helped. Illinois is a lot more liberal than Louisiana. I'm not getting shut down for anything like that." I shook my head.

"Why do all the facilities have to be in Louisiana?" LeBlanc asked.

"For now, the starter ones will be, so we can keep an eye on the protocols and adjust them as needed. Perfect the system. I'm open to expansion. But one thing at a time," I said.

LeBlanc looked over at Brimlow.

"No pressure. It was nice to meet you. Bottom line, I need some good consultants—medical, psychological, and organizational. If you don't want to work with me, fine. If you're interested, okay—we can see if it's a fit. I don't make any promises, but my staff will be well compensated, because I want to keep the best talent, and I want people to feel safe in their jobs to be able to focus on helping people because they're not worried about money." I turned to Brimlow. "But no more sharing the plan without asking me first. I need to control the information."

"Sorry," he said.

I turned and left the office with Gunnar on my heels.

"The nun mobile will be tricked out, right? Sunroof and leather?" Gunnar asked.

"Oh, yeah. They're getting every button, bell, and whistle. If they complain, you put one of those decals for the new business on the side so it's a business vehicle and tell them we need the tax deduction. Then, they can't complain." I winked at him.

"That LeBlanc guy was checking you out," Gunnar said.

"Please, he's full of himself," I said.

"He's hot. You noticed." Gunnar grinned.

"I noticed. You noticed, too. You ask him out. He's proud and arrogant. We'll talk to some of his patients before we hire him. If he's even interested. I need to see his true bedside manner first."

"Get in bed and make him show you." Gunnar laughed as we trudged through the parking structure.

I rolled my eyes at him. "You're hysterical. You need a boyfriend badly."

"We both do. I expect we'll hire some hot male nurses, too. Throw me a bone," he said.

"Round them up and have them apply for the jobs. Help yourself and help the cause if that's what you want. I can't do all the work," I said.

"Oh, God, Sunday School flashback. God helps those who helps themselves." Gunnar opened my car door.

"You said it, I didn't. Thankfully, no one forced the Chapter and verse memorization on me." I hopped in the car. "What color car do you buy for nuns? Black or white would be so cliché."

A Personal Note from Ivy...

Dear Reader,

I always knew Voodoo was real but zombies?? And Daryl Dixon didn't come to save us. I'm so disappointed. The stripper almost made up for it.

Of course, De's brother being around is a nice bonus, too. So many cute men, and she's spending time with a guy who was nearly dead and let Death use his body. I mean, it's a nice body and all, but I need to get her a life...ya know, on this Earth with a living man.

And don't even get me started on these kids today. Hoodoo? A teen messing with that? Parents, sometimes, you have to tell your kids no and take their phone away.

Don't worry, I'm having a Voodoo Priestess, a Catholic priest, and a Shaman bless the club and keep the evil and bullets far away!

Now, do you have all of our adventures???

Book 1 A Mansion, A Drag Queen, And A New Job: https://www.amazon.com/gp/product/B00QSNV82C

Book 2 A Club, An Imposter, And A Competition: https://www.amazon.com/gp/product/B00SKIPAJ0

Book 3 A Bar, A Brother, And A Ghost Hunt: https://www.amazon.com/gp/product/B01LXNSZHL

Book 5 is in the works...all I can say is there are way too many hot undead men in New Orleans!

Sign up for the Newsletter to get all the updates! https://app.mailerlite.com/webforms/landing/o6l4fo

Now, I need to go. Gotta a date with that cute stripper ;) Only kidding!

Love & Jewels,

Ivy

About the Author

A loyal Chicago girl who loves deep dish pizza, the Cubs, and the Lake, CC Dragon is fascinated by mysteries, sleuthing, as well as the supernatural.

CC loves creating characters, especially amateur sleuths who solve crimes in their spare time. A coffee and chocolate addict who loves fast cars, she's still looking for a hero who likes to cook and clean...so she can write more!

Website: http://www.ccdragon.com

Facebook: https://www.facebook.com/ccdragonauthor

Twitter: https://twitter.com/authorccdragon

Blog: https://www.ccdragon.wordpress.com